Immigrant Me

& Other Short Stories

2nd Edition

By

C. Osvaldo Gomez

Printed in the United States of America

First printing, 2016

ISBN 978-1-365-56198-6

Lulu Press, Inc
www.lulu.com

Dedication

I dedicate this book to immigrants all over the world.
Your hustle, hard work, and struggle for survival are
unfortunately only comprehensible to other
immigrants. Without your contributions mighty
nations would collapse.

Acknowledgement

This book wouldn't have been possible without the help of many. First I'd like to thank the many immigrants who inspired some of the characters in this book. *Gracias Joel, y Jorge por ser de los mejores jardineros en Oceanside CA, a las señoras del* Maid Brigade, *Maria y Lupita, y a los jornaleros de las esquinas, especialmente a los que se juntan en* North Santa Fe Road y Melrose Drive. Without their experiences in America, I couldn't have made these stories come alive.

I'd also like to thank the good people at the now defunct www.writerstype.com for selecting some of these stories as winners (The Curb, Challenger, and The Freight Train) and for online publication. Also for editing the stories for free as part of the publication process. Thank you also for putting me in contact with John P. Doyle who I hired as my editor for the remaining stories in this book.

Lastly, I'd like to thank my parents, Carlos and Teresa, for their support throughout this process. I was too young to remember many of the events that took place prior to and during our immigration from Mexico. Their recollections helped me fill in the gaps.

Preface

It's 2016 and the issue of immigration in America is still a conundrum no one knows for sure what to do with. Syrian refugees have spooked Western democracies to the point of irrational fear. Indeed, the fear of Muslims and Mexicans won Donald Trump the greatest prize in all the free world: The U.S. Presidency. Building the wall along the border has become the solution many Americans believe will keep Mexico from sending "people that have lot's of problems." What's unfortunate is not that Americans don't feel safe with an unsecured border. I think everyone can agree this is a top national concern. The tragedy is that groups of people had to be vilified throughout an electoral process.

The contributions of immigrants and the children of immigrants have been forgotten in America. Our own President-Elect is the son and grandson of immigrants who embodied the American entrepreneurial spirit while living in the Land of Opportunity. That didn't seem to matter. Apparently, only European immigrants come here to fully take advantage of the wonderful opportunities this country offers everyone. Of course this is a myth. Immigrants who have come to this country from all over the world have started businesses, paid their taxes, and contributed greatly to American society.

I wrote this book for a singular purpose: to give Americans an idea of who Latino immigrants are. We are hustlers in the best of ways. We outwork many people not out of spite or competition, but rather because we have been given a blessing to live in the best country in the world, and we don't want to squander that. Our work for many of us keeps us from the danger of having to return to our country of birth and leave all of this unique freedom behind. We don't make excuses and we don't complain like the average American. We know how good we have it and are appreciative to the nth degree. This book relates our struggles and hardships. It also depicts the circumstances that cause us to consider leaving all we know behind, our families and friends, to give our children a better chance at life.

I put this book out to market in 2013 without much thought. It had just been a finalist (top 13) in the 2012 Grace Notes Publishing: Discovering the Undiscovered fiction book contest. Like many beginning authors, I thought I could do the marketing on my own. Big mistake. The first eBook version of the book only sold about 200 copies in a year. I spent less than $50 on advertisement, and used free Facebook posting as my main strategy to get the word out.

This re-launch of sorts includes some actual front matter. My amateur self had forgotten to include a Copyright, Dedication, and Acknowledgement page in the original. I've also added a bonus story, The Freight Train, at the end. I intend on being more aggressive in the marketing of this 2nd edition to get this book out there. I have to defeat obscurity because I know that what I have here is a great product that needs to be in the hands of many people. I know you will enjoy these memorable stories and they will leave you with an unshakeable impression for the rest of your life. Thank-you for buying this book!

C. Osvaldo Gomez

Table of Contents

The Curb

Today will be better, Jesus said to himself. He stood confidently along the curb with the others. It was cold, damn cold. The men huddled close to each other, but not too close. It was around 6:00 a.m. on a Saturday in November on the outskirts of Fallbrook, California.

"Hey *Pancho*," one of the Oaxacans said. "How's your family?"

"Bien," another Oaxacan said. "And yours?"

Damn Oaxaqueños, Jesus thought. So many of them.

He took a good look at the lot, trying to see each as they'd be seen by the locals. Only a few were of average American height. Most were short, dark, and stout. They looked strong, standing with broad shoulders and barrel chests.

Jesus was from Sinaloa, a rugged northern state on the west coast of Mexico. At five-foot-ten, he was taller than most of the men looking for work. He was a well-built man. His fair complexion was tinged red from days burned by the sun. Jesus was good with a hammer. He preferred housing and cement work to landscaping. Landscaping was not his strength. Of course the Oaxacans were good at everything.

The cold air stung at the back of his throat. It was easier to inhale through the nostrils. The morning sun began to rise above the hill that was behind the workers. Most of the men had their hands in their jacket pockets. This was one way they sized each other up. Those who considered themselves better than others stayed still. They didn't move side-to-side, or put their hands near their mouths and blow like a *maricon*, a faggot. They were *machos*.

Jesus daydreamed, remembering the last time he saw his family. It was a beautiful May morning in Culiacan City. Anxious about the trip north, he didn't sleep well the night before. Out of concern, his wife, Celia Maria, didn't either.

"Here are your eggs with beans," Celia Maria said. "How many tortillas would you like?"

"Just two, *Vieja*," Jesus said, noticing the sadness in her voice. They'd only been married fourteen months. Despite being a recently wed couple, he affectionately called her, *Vieja*, or Old Love.

Celia Maria was more educated than her three older brothers. She was the only one in her family to finish *Preparatoria* or High School. Jesus, like Celia Maria's brothers, had worked since he could remember. "The books didn't stick," he said when asked why he didn't finish school. At seven, he dropped out. He shined shoes at the bus terminal to help his father put food on the table. As a teen, Jesus had stints working with his brother building houses. He worked at a PEMEX gas station in between construction projects. At twenty, he was hired at the Wrangler plant. Then his luck ran out.

The unemployment streak of eight months had struck at his manhood. His responsibility was to provide for his family no matter what. Being twenty one-years-old was no excuse. He was a grown Mexican man. Jesus maintained a routine during the downturn: early breakfast, and out to look for work around Culiacan. Each day he came back with little to show. On a good day he made sixty pesos, or six U.S. dollars. On a bad day he came home empty handed. To support the two of them, Celia Maria had to find work of her own. Doing her a favor, a family friend hired Celia Maria as a cashier in an *abarrotes*, or general store. Eight months into her pregnancy, Celia Maria had to quit.

Once the cold stopped being a challenge the men moved in place passing the time, staying limber in case they needed to run. They were in a foreign land and shared a common pain. Some felt a strain in their hearts, a constant fear of getting caught by *la migra*. Others felt a throb in their heads, a daily migraine of shame that could only be relieved by the analgesic of finding work. This was Jesus' first season away from home, and though he was surrounded every morning by familiar faces, he was lonely. He longed for a warm embrace from his *Vieja*. The sound of an engine coming up the hill snapped Jesus from his pleasant reverie.

The Oaxacans quickly lined up at the edge of the curb, placing themselves in the best spot. Damn me to hell! Jesus thought. These guys are professionals. He ran to where they stood. The vehicle came closer and closer, eventually passing by. In return for their canine-like interest, the men got a look of disgust from the elderly man driving the car. Puffed up chests deflated, and heads dropped several inches. There would be no *trabajo* for now. Jesus walked back slowly to his favorite spot near two lush shrubs. The gringos water everything, he said to himself. Drip line tubing snaked along the hill. He turned around, admiring a green field across the road.

Fallbrook was a great place for *jornaleros*, or day laborers. Suburban dwellings mixed with ranch homes in the valley below. The hillside on E. Mission Road was a popular gathering spot for *jornaleros*. The majority of them walked there each day. Jesus noticed a cottontail racing across the field. I bet these

Oaxaqueños know how to skin them, he thought. He wasn't used to their strange language yet, their coarse Spanish and exotic *Zapotec* dialect. He imagined them living in a jungle village somewhere in Oaxaca, each owning a machete, subsisting off their crops and small game. *Indios*, he said to himself each time he heard them get into a Zapotecan squabble. Still, they were his countrymen, and better than having Central Americans around. The Central Americans came to the curb once in a while, gathering in the space the Mexicans didn't want. They clumped like turds, laughing at their own *hijo de la gran puta* (son of the great whore) jokes.

Hours passed and the morning faded away. Still no one came seeking hands. With the start of the holiday season, demand for cheap labor had diminished, and it was almost time for Jesus to head back to Culiacan. Soon he and his *paisanos* would take part in a reverse migration, like salmon swimming back to their birth streams. Jesus imagined Celia Maria plump and round, carrying his future son. He'd spoken to her two days before, using a 7-11 $5 calling card at a pay phone.

"How's *el Norte*?" she asked.

"A little slow. *No hay mucho trabajo. Vieja,* how about we name him, Jesus?"

"No more, 'Jesus'," Celia Maria said jokingly. "There's already too many."

Jesus' stomach growled at him. He looked at his watch: 11:45 a.m. Time for lunch, he thought. He reached into his backpack, grabbing two burritos wrapped in foil, along with a water bottle filled with tap. Before leaving for work, he had overheated the bean burritos in a microwave, and they were still warm. He found it difficult living in the garage of someone's house, not having access to a kitchen. He was only allowed a microwave and small refrigerator. He didn't, however, have much experience in the kitchen. His mother had taken care of him most of his life. As a momma's boy, he'd paid careful attention to her repeated words of wisdom: "Marry a woman who knows how to cook!"

He bit into one of the burritos and glanced at the other men as he chewed. They were eating their meals too. The better off ones had steak tacos. The not so fortunate had canned peaches. He finished his first burrito and stopped eating, saving the other for later. It was warm by noon. The workers did their best to stay comfortable, unbuttoning their shirts and unzipping their jackets. Caps and hats covered the asphalt with beak-like shadows.

Jesus' mind began to wander again. He recalled the two weeks he spent in Tijuana with a cousin, trying to cross the line, "*la línea*," as immigrants call it. He got caught twice. Each time his Coyote mistimed the approach across the border through the rows of cars. He was spotted once crouched in between the checkpoint and the vehicles entering Mexico. The second time he tried running across, but was chased down by a Border Patrol agent and his dog.

The heck with it, Jesus said to himself, walking back into Mexico after the second foiled attempt. He decided to try crossing through the hills around Mexicali. "Crossing through the hills will be treacherous," his cousin said. "The terrain is dangerous. You'll also need to look out for gangs." If Jesus was lucky, he'd just be robbed. He could be beaten, or worse, forced to work as a mule for a drug cartel. Surprisingly, it had been neither. He made it across safely.

Jesus heard another vehicle coming up the hill. This time he was ready with his backpack on his shoulder. He got into position beside the Oaxacans. Their numbers monopolized the coveted space on the curb again. A truck with an empty bed stopped suddenly before the men. Shouts of "here!" overwhelmed the driver. Multiple arms reached for the sky, begging for selection. Jesus attempted to get into the gringo's line of sight. There were so many men trying to do the same.

The hand of god, the hand of god...Jesus repeated in his head. He had grown religious away from home, keeping a worn-out Catholic bible near his mattress. The bible was a gift from his cousin in Tijuana. Every night, he read from the New Testament, praying for his wife's health before falling asleep. "You and you!" the white man said from inside the cabin, pointing at two Oaxacans. The Oaxacans jumped onto the back of the truck like excited dogs. The pair smiled victoriously, looking back at their dejected counterparts. Off they went. *¡Chinga su madre!* Jesus said to himself.

Back on the curb, Jesus passed the time tossing small rocks up the incline. He kneeled, picked a handful off the ground, and from a catcher's position threw as hard as he could. Jesus loved baseball. Sinaloa being a northern state, many youths played baseball instead of soccer.

During his teenage years, Jesus played in a team representing his municipality. He was the starting catcher, and was considered among the best in Culiacan. He traveled to Los Mochis and Mazatlan, playing against their best. He fared well. At nineteen, Jesus was offered a chance to try out for *Los Cañeros de Los Mochis*, a professional team in Mexico's Pacific league.

14

Just like his experience at school, the day at the tryout was an utter disappointment. During base-stealing drills, he overthrew and missed his mark to second base. He failed to stop errant pitches to the mound. At bat, he showed little power. It was the worst performance of his life. Jesus was not asked to come back.

"That's not like you," Celia Maria said, listening to Jesus tell her about the tryout. "What happened?"

"I get really nervous during tests," he said.

After tossing rocks, Jesus sat on the edge of the sidewalk. He looked at his watch again: 2:55 p.m. Some of the men were leaving, giving up for the day. Only a few hours of daylight remained, the winter workday cut short by the sun's early set. *Pinches maricones*, Jesus thought. They give up too easily. I'm staying another hour.

In six months, Jesus had made more money working in the U.S. than he had the entire previous year in Mexico. With the money he sent home, Celia Maria was able to buy a crib and baby clothes. He kept just enough money to feed himself and pay his monthly rent for the garage.

At 3:15 p.m. Jesus heard the sound of another engine coming up the hill. There were few men left to compete for the curb's best realty. A double cab Tundra stopped in front of the men.

"I need a good rooster!" the voice said in Spanish from inside.

"*¡Aquí está su gallo!*" or "Here is your rooster!" Jesus said, leaping forward. *"El mejor gallo de Culiacan, Sinaloa."*

Some men let out a howl while others laughed.

"Okay, you," the man said, appreciating Jesus' pride. "Get inside."

Jesus didn't hesitate. Quickly he grabbed the handle and opened the door. Once inside he felt an inner peace deep down to his bones, and his muscles relaxed.

"The boss had to get rid of a guy and we need another to finish the job," the man said, with a Mexican-American accent. "You know how to lay concrete?"

"*Si,*" Jesus said. "I used to do it in Culiacan."

Not much else was said. Jesus was used to the silence. Why get to know someone, or even ask a person their name, when there's no certainty of ever meeting again?

At the job site, Jesus worked his ass off. He was a machine. The Mexican-American middleman didn't have to give him instructions. Jesus helped pour and level concrete. He was an artist on his knees with the hand trowel. "He makes it look so easy," the contractor said aloud, noticing Jesus work.

The crew worked until they could no longer see. They gathered their things, and left one by one. The Mexican-American, the contractor's right-hand man, put tools in the back of his truck with Jesus' help. "I'll drive you back," he said to Jesus.

They drove off from the job site, feeling tired and hungry.

"My name's Michael," he said, breaking the silence. "You know, *Miguel*, but here they call me, Michael."

"Jesus."

"Jesus," Michael said, "the boss really likes your work. He said you're a hard worker."

"*O, si,*" Jesus said, humbled. The truck stopped where each morning men waited with hope. The place was dark and vacated.

"Here's your money," Michael said. "Sixty."

"That's good." Not bad for three hours, he thought.

"Listen, Jesus," Michael said, "the boss wants you to work for him. Tomorrow we're going to another house. You interested?"

"Yes, of course."

"Okay, perfect. Be here in the morning and I'll come get you."

"Sure," Jesus said full of gratitude.

Jesus waived at the truck with his free hand, the other hand firmly holding the cash. Michael returned the gesture and drove off. Jesus descended into the valley below en route to his garage. What luck, he said to himself. He began to imagine what he'd do with the money. He considered building an extra room; an addition to the one-bedroom house Celia Maria's family gave them as a marriage gift. The house was small, less than 800 square feet, with a tiny kitchen, a bathroom without a bathtub, and the single room where living and sleeping took place. Maybe a bigger kitchen for Celia Maria? he thought. It's going to be a great Christmas.

The next day Jesus walked vigorously to the curb, getting there right about six. A trio of Oaxacans huddled with their coffees in hand. Jesus had packed for a long day, three bean and rice burritos, and two water bottles full of water. It was cold again. Smoke puffed out of the mouths of the men. Jesus stood around, seeing more and more men arrive, greeting one another, and beginning small talk. The place was coming alive. Time passed with Jesus standing around, keeping his ears open for the sound of a truck engine. He looked at his watch: 7:15 a.m.

He'll probably be here soon, Jesus thought. He wondered what Michael had meant by, "be here in the morning." He figured Michael meant sometime before noon. Jesus was there, and ready to go. That's all that mattered.

At around eight Jesus heard the growl of an engine. He walked onto the street to get a better look. Maybe it's Miguel, he said to himself. Meanwhile, the men arranged themselves, like dancers waiting on the stage before the music. Jesus walked hesitantly toward the cluster. It doesn't look like Miguel's truck, he thought. The truck came to a slow stop. "Three!" the white man inside said, holding up three fingers. There was a scramble. Jesus was confused. If I get picked, Miguel might come by and not see me here, he said to himself. "You, you, and you," the man said decisively, picking three other Mexicans.

At around nine-thirty Jesus got hungry. He ate one of his burritos and drank some water. At ten-thirty he sat along the curb, thinking about Celia Maria and their future son. He considered naming his son, Michael. Jesus was sure that at any minute, Michael would arrive and drive him to the job site, where he would work hard, real hard, make the boss and his new friend glad they put him on the crew.

Noon came and passed. The men around Jesus began to eat their lunches. Jesus gathered some small rocks from the ground behind him, put some in his pocket, and kept a handful in his left hand, his glove hand. He sat back on the curb, looking at the field in the foreground once more. He threw across the street, aiming at bushes and large rocks.

The commotion stirred a cottontail out of its den. Unsure of what to be afraid of, the animal looked around before making a move. Jesus took quick aim and fired off at the rabbit. The throw was short by a few inches. Startled, the rabbit instinctively took flight, running and leaping across the field until it reached another hole to its den where it disappeared from view.

"Not gonna eat, *compadre*?" a chubby Oaxacan asked, squatting nearby with a taco in his hand.

"No," Jesus said. "I lost my appetite."

Sara

"Hey, you," Mark said.

"Well, hi," Jennifer said. "Nice to see ya."

They embraced at the door, pulling back to give each other a kiss. Jennifer, blonde with an athletic figure, smiled, allowing her guest to come inside. Mark, a well-built Latino male, with a soft face and dimples on each cheek, returned the gesture.

Jennifer's body felt tingly all over. This being her third rendezvous with Mark, nervousness had given way to a feeling of excitement that controlled her body. She wore a thin red tank-top and her favorite shorts, exposing her best features: voluptuous breasts and firm legs. Mark stared at her legs as she turned around to close the door.

The shutters and curtains were closed. The house was still and cozy. Sara, the hired help, had been sent on several errands, and she had left enough food in Shiloh's dog bowl to last him several hours. Shiloh, a two-year-old, long-haired, golden, Pekingese, strutted about Jennifer's feet.

The sound of Shiloh's small nails striking the hardwood floor caught Mark's attention. "Hi, boy," he said, kneeling to pet Shiloh. "Look, he's not barking anymore." Jennifer picked Shiloh up, cuddled him, and gave him a peck on his head. "Good boy," she said, placing the dog on the floor. She walked further inside. Mark followed.

Jennifer took a right at the split, stepping inside the formal dining room. A large cabinet and bar stood at the edge of the room. The cabinet was stocked with enough liquors and liqueurs to make a drunk salivate.

"Would you like a drink?" Jennifer asked, opening a bottle and pouring herself a glass.

"Sure," Mark said. "I'll have what you're having."

"Courvoisier," she said. "My husband has seen one too many rap videos."

"What does he do for a living?"

"He runs a hedge fund in Frisco," she said regrettably. "Some sort of investment hot-shot."

Mark nodded casually, feeling inadequate. He worked as a trainer at 24-Hour Fitness where he'd met Jennifer. "He must be a busy guy."

"Too busy," she said with bitterness.

Jennifer and Albert had been married for five years. They had yet to have a serious talk about children. Albert had given little thought to becoming a father. Business dominated all of his priorities. Jennifer had always wanted to be a mother.

Albert had suggested to Jennifer that she go to the gym. He was tired of listening to Jennifer complain: "I'm so bored at home, Honey," she told him repeatedly. "You should workout during the day," he finally said one day. While exercising, Jennifer noticed Mark helping a client. "Honey, I'm gonna need a trainer," she said to Albert. Provided she didn't start nagging again, Albert was willing to pay for her sessions.

Jennifer finished her drink. She noticed Mark stroking the side of his half empty cup. "Give me your cup," she said impatiently. She grabbed it, came around the bar, and left the room. While Jennifer rinsed both cups in the kitchen, Mark inspected the collection of booze. Jenifer placed the cups in the dishwasher among the others, getting rid of the evidence. She hurried back to the dining room. She took Mark by the hand and led him out of the room, moving things along. Mark had turned out to be a great lay, a correct prediction she'd first made back at the gym. Someday she'd have to turn him away. She'd do it gently to spare his feelings.

Albert was nothing like Mark. *He* was all about control. Luck, success, and superior intellect had developed his huge ego. At Morgan Stanley, Albert was a rocket: security analyst at twenty-five, seduced by a lucrative offer into a position as portfolio manager at thirty two, and then onto running money at his own fund, LENNAR GROUP. He liked his women beautiful, well dressed, and submissive.

Jennifer pulled Mark down the hallway to the door of the master bedroom. Controlling Mark turned Jennifer on. Mark played along. He liked his women feisty and confident. She flung the door open, turning around in the doorway to face him. She took her tank-top off, pulling him closer toward her, and allowed her breasts to rest on his pectorals. She slowly kissed his lips, caressing the back of his neck with her left hand. Her right hand crept inside his tight shirt, and she circled his belly button with her index finger. Her fingers climbed the ladder of his chiseled abdomen. Locked as one, the two stepped inside the room, slamming the door shut.

Aside from keeping the kitchen clean, Sara's responsibilities included the laundry, feeding Shiloh, cleaning the bathrooms, and picking up around the house. But her most important task of the day was cooking dinner. Jennifer was a horrible cook. She hated cooking. Sara decided the previous day to cook Albert's favorite Mexican dinner, *Mole Poblano*, chicken smothered in a thick and rich, chocolate-tinged sauce. Sara's mother had taught her how to make the dish back in Mexico City.

Preparing the meal reminded Sara of good times with her mother. She'd become depressed after her mother's death, from the angst of not having been able to be at her side. In the late eighties, Sara had made frequent trips to Mexico, but increasing security at the border made it too risky to keep trying to cross illegally. Immigrating to the U.S. for the first time in late '84 was the biggest mistake of her life. If only I'd left in '82—she'd ponder, tormenting herself— and qualified for Reagan's amnesty.

Sara hurried about the aisles of Albertson's in Palo Alto, as quickly as her short legs would allow. She stood five-foot-tall, above average for a Mexican woman. She pushed the cart along, standing out like a rotten vegetable on display. Her dark, burnished tone, tied black hair, and cheap dress perked the curiosity of a middle age white woman rolling her cart in the opposite direction. As a person of color, Sara was used to the attention she got while shopping in Palo Alto. She passed quickly around an elderly man in an electric wheelchair, surprising him.

The bedroom was humid, full of air charged with pheromones. The sheets snaked around the naked bodies of the lovers. Jennifer woke up, looking at the digital clock on Albert's nightstand. She sat up suddenly on the bed.

"Mark, get up," she said. "It's almost four."

"Is it your husband?" he asked, still groggy.

"No, Sara," she said. "She's due back soon. Albert gets home around seven most nights."

"Oh, okay." He got out of bed, staring at the clutter of clothes and shoes on the floor. "Is she an illegal?"

"I have no idea," she said. "Albert hired her before we married."

She began removing the sheets and pulled the comforter back to aerate its interior lining.

"Must be nice having a maid," Mark said.

"Sure," she said sarcastically, "she's great."

"Tell me more about her later," Mark said fully dressed.

He gave Jennifer a kiss. Jennifer's lips had lost their zeal. The passion was gone and her mind was elsewhere, on her husband.

"Make sure Sara doesn't see you," she said.

Sara saved a chunk of time at the grocery store, buying the ingredients for the *mole* sauce the day before on her way to work. The *Super-Mercado* on Story Road in East San Jose was better stocked than any Latino food store in Palo Alto. Sara approached the Lennar's place, a 2800 square foot single-family home in the Palo Alto Hills. The late-nineties home was in a neighborhood Sara believed to be perfect for Mr. *Alberto*. Other urban sophisticates and executives like her boss lived there, enjoying the peace and quiet "The City" couldn't offer.

She planned to make dinner first. She wanted it ready by the time Mr. *Alberto* came home. She'd have at least thirty minutes to clean up around the house while the chicken and sauce simmered on the skillet. The brakes of her 2000 Ford Escort began to screech a few houses before her destination. Mark sat in his car with his music turned up loud.

Not again, Sara thought, as Mark pulled away from the house.

Sara had decided against letting her boss know of the affair. The situation was complicated. There was no guarantee that Mr. *Alberto* would believe her, and that would leave her wide open for the vixen to take a stab at her. But what if Mr. Alberto finds out about the affair and fires me for not telling him? she thought. She put her mind in a further frenzy by recalling an event at the Lennar's during their third year of marriage.

She was doing laundry at the time. She went into the Lennar's bedroom to pull the sheets off. She began bundling the top sheet after removing the comforter, exposing a coiled red thong underneath. Jennifer had been away on a ladies-only trip. This isn't one of mises Lennar's thongs, Sara thought. She heard the wheels of Jennifer's suitcase being rolled toward the master bedroom. Jennifer had come home unexpectedly. Sara snatched the thong from the mattress and put it in her apron pocket, moments before Jennifer entered the room. "Huelcom bak, mises Lennar," she'd said, relieved. Prior to putting Mr. *Alberto's* pants inside the washer, she checked the pockets, and found yet another clue: "…San Francisco's best call girls," read the business card she held in her hand.

Sara walked into the kitchen from a door at the side of the house. The kitchen was empty, but she soon livened-it up with her hustle and bustle. She hummed a Mexican tune, *Cielito Lindo*, to get herself going and forget things on her mind. She knew where she could find mises Lennar if she needed her, inside her room getting ready.

Jennifer's evening routine included showering, putting on a nice outfit, and fixing her hair before Albert came home. Albert would often invite associates to the house without telling her. He expected his wife always ready to entertain company.

Sara finished preparing the meal and left the kitchen to set the dinning room table. After this, she picked-up, dusted, and wiped, room-by-room, oblivious to anything else. She moved quietly, almost undetectable, and tried not to interrupt mises Lennar. The last thing she needed is to be on mises Lennar's bad side.

Albert arrived at his castle, parking his vehicle inside the garage. Before opening the door he looked at himself in the rear view mirror, checking for rouge on his Phillips-Van Heusen shirt collar. He stepped out, emptied his pockets, smelled his shoulders with his jacket off, and put the jacket back on. He walked inside the house. The aroma of the *mole* chicken struck him like the scent of a candy store. He went straight to the kitchen.

"Hi, Sara."

"Hi, mister *Alberto*," she said.

"Smells delicious," he said, opening the tops of pots and pans on the stove and admiring the colorful food.

"Gracias."

"I'm starving," he said. "Can you please go get Mrs. Lennar and tell her I'm home?"

"Yes, mister *Alberto*."

Sara walked to the master bedroom and knocked on the door.

"Mises Lennar," she said. "Mister *Alberto* is home."

"Okay," Jennifer said. "Thank-you, Sara. I'll be right out."

Jennifer left the bedroom wearing an evening dress and heels, her hair let down, light make-up highlighting her gorgeous facial features. Sara deferred to Jennifer, allowing her to make her grand entrance into the kitchen. She moved like a model. Before following her, Sara stood incredulous for a moment in the hallway. She's good, Sara thought, not a trace of guilt.

"Hi, honey," Jennifer said.

Albert smiled.

"Wine, dear?" he held an extra glass in his hand.

Sara waited at the edge of the kitchen. She enjoyed watching the refined interaction between them. She'd seen it before in other homes and wondered if this was typical of rich couples.

"Sure, honey," she said.

Albert poured her a cupful of a vintage Napa Valley merlot.

Sara was distracted by a noise coming from the hallway behind her: Shiloh's growling. The dog held something in its mouth. Sara's jaw dropped when she noticed what it was.

"¡Shiloh, no!" she said, intercepting the dog steps away from the kitchen and instinctively taking the item from its mouth.

"Is everything alright, Sara?" Albert asked, coming out the kitchen to see about the commotion.

"Yes, mister *Alberto*," she said, crumbling Jennifer's moist panties into a fist and crossing her arms behind her.

Jennifer had accidentally kicked her underwear below the bed, rushing to get at Mark.

"Come here Shiloh!" Albert said.

Sara could've held the panties out for Albert to see, planting a seed of suspicion in him. Jennifer wasn't a messy person. She never left her clothes within Shiloh's reach. Sara could've also asked mister *Alberto* for money prematurely, to replenish his dwindling supply of liquor. Little by little Sara could've left clues for Albert. But she liked working for mister *Alberto*.

Sara had learned a lot from her previous experiences as a maid. The biggest lesson she'd learned was to not get involved. Twice she'd gotten fired as a result of interfering. The first time, Sara had discovered where her former boss' son, Luke, stashed his marijuana. She'd led the teen's mother, Amy, right to where Luke kept the contraband in his room. Luke was disciplined, and a few days later, he got his revenge. Luke hid his mother's pearl earrings in Sara's apron. At breakfast that morning, Luke intentionally dropped a spoon on the floor. Sara bent down to pick it up and out came the earrings.

Another time she was fired for taking Breanna, a sixteen-year-old, to Planned Parenthood. She was working for the Johnson's at the time. Breanna, the Johnson's daughter, ditched school with her boyfriend, having sex at the house. "I think I'm pregnant," Breanna said to Sara, confiding in her. She begged Sara to take her to Planned Parenthood. Sara drove Breanna to the nearest clinic. On their way home, the two were seen by a friend of the Johnson's. Sara was let go the next day. From then on Sara vowed never to get caught up in a family's affairs.

Sara joined her employers in the kitchen.
"Sara," Albert said, "things look great."
"Yes, Sara," Jennifer said.
"Have we ever told you what a great job you do around here?" Albert asked.
"It-sa nating, mister *Alberto*," Sara said with humility plastered on her face.

Immigrant Me

I had not seen the ocean before I visited Santa Cruz in '84. It was a Friday in mid April. The morning when we set out from San Jose had been gloomy and gray. A persistent fog, the type that burns off in the afternoon, had smothered the South Bay overnight. Beyond our valley the bus ride to our destination was difficult, uphill on the treacherous Highway 17. As we climbed over the mountain the switchbacks made me queasy. I suffer from carsickness. I would've puked, if it weren't for the distracting chatter and excitement around me.

The bus hummed along, slowing in shifts between gears. We stared in awe at the tall redwoods and forest outside our windows. I imagined an amazing scene, seeing a deer along the road feeding on the brush. If I discovered the animal and pointed it out before anyone else, I'd be the hero of the journey early on, I thought. Most of us had never seen a deer, or been outside our neighborhoods.

The bus ride through Scotts Valley as we neared Santa Cruz was like being in another planet. Large rustic-looking homes sat on tracts of green lawns with enough running room for me and my friends to play soccer. At the apartment complex where I lived the grass was dead and we played on the street.

We came onto Ocean Street from Highway 17. We were finally in Santa Cruz. I looked at the strange sights before me: quaint shops, everyone wearing long shorts and sandals. The beach town, with its slender avenues, was coming alive. I was overwhelmed by the Americana. Small U.S. flags hung on windows and doors, surfers walked with their boards, and skaters did tricks on street corners. My Mexican existence got shocked. I no longer felt the comfort of my world. The familiar grounds of my *barrio* and school, all I'd ever known, cowered in the back of my mind. On Beach Street we got our first glimpse of the beach. I'd seen desert sand back in Chihuahua, but this sand had an irregular blue boundary that retreated and re-emerged, life giving, not callous.

As we approached the parking lot of the beach boardwalk, you could hear screaming across the street rising and falling away. It was the sounds of the roller coaster. We parked and stood up eagerly on our cramped legs. Our teacher, Mrs. Garcia, popped our balloons. "Stay in your seat," she said. "I have to tell you the park rules…"

Mrs. Garcia was a second mother to us. She was young, perhaps early thirties, short, dark brown skin, with typical Latina curves, full breasts and hips. There weren't many dark brown people where I'd grown up in Chihuahua: Meoqui, a small town forty-five minutes south of the state capital. The *pueblo* was named after General Pedro Meoqui who died in battle fighting the French in 1865. Most of the people of Meoqui were fair complexioned. So was I. I'd been called a little *güerito*—a blond, fair skinned person—all of my life.

Being fair-skinned and blond had given me identity, and a sense of superiority among my friends back in Mexico. *"Que güerito esta su hijo, señora,"* or "You're son is so blond, madam," adults would tell my mother, patting my head, making me feel special. It was like a gift from God. I could pass for a white kid when in need. The need materialized in Ciudad Juarez, summer of '83. I was six at the time.

"When we get across, I want you and your sister to start skipping, throwing rocks, whatever," said the Coyote on whose shoulders I sat as we crossed a canal of the Rio Grande. "Should be very easy for the two of you *güeritos*," he said a little further along, huffing and puffing with water up to his knees.

I was competitive by nature. This too was a godsend. The games in class were timed. Quickest to complete the addition worksheet got a star. "I'm finished!" was my call of victory. So sweet to scream it out, please the teacher, and rub it in the face of the other kids. I won many math battles in class. Outside the boys battled each other: fastest to the wall starting at the swings, best at Four Square, and other games. The lean kids like Jorge, Pedro, and me beat everyone else at sports.

Things were different in America. Brown-skinned Mexicans like Jorge and Pedro were in the majority. They made fun of *güero*s like me. They called me names like "whiteboy" and "gringo." Then there was Lucas, a Mexican-American, who spoke few Spanish words. Jorge and Pedro called him a name I'd never heard before, "pocho." Lucas was pudgy, pot-bellied, had droopy cheeks, and bit his bottom lip when nervous. He was like our mascot.

My friends and I hated being separated. "Do you speak Spanish?" the teacher asked out-loud every day after lunch, prompting the class. Since Lucas didn't, he had to follow the aide with the one or two black and white kids in the class. They belonged to the, *"Un Poco Nada Mas,"* or "Just A Little" group. Jorge, Pedro, myself, the rest of the newcomers, were placed in the, *"¡Si, Como No!"* or "Yes, Of Course!" group. The teacher worked with us on improving our elementary level Spanish. Bilingual Education was in its heyday.

We got off the bus in Santa Cruz and breathed the clean air. The smell of beach air and seaweed was distinctive, just like San Jose smog and the dumpster smells of my apartment complex. I wore shorts, sandals, and a t-shirt, as we were told to do in the Spanish letter sent to our families. The sun was out. Good thing too. Santa Cruz was cooler than I'd thought it would be. Jorge, Pedro, Lucas, and I walked up the hill into the park, planning how we would spend our day. We'd heard about the arcade and some of the rides from Mrs. Garcia.

We walked onto the boardwalk and quickly noticed we weren't alone. Multiple schools from the South Bay had chosen the same day to have a fieldtrip. We stood still for a few seconds, getting our bearings. Everywhere kids ran to the rides, cackling in English. "Let's go to Loggers Revenge!" one white kid yelled to his friend.

Jorge, our unelected leader, strongest and most aggressive, good with the girls, decided what we should do first. "To the arcade!" he said. Playing video games was the least scary thing to do. We were new to the park. We had no idea what it took to get on a ride, where to get food, or even where to find the arcade. The American kids went about with ease, their sense of entitlement, and their fear of nothing, made us jealous.

Ms. Pac-Man, Space Invaders, and Frogger were beginning to tire us out. We played the same games at the liquor store and Laundromat back home. We beat a few gringo kids at Space Invader and enjoyed erasing their initials on the highest score list. "Stupid wetbacks," a blond, blue-eyed lanky kid said, walking away. We didn't need to know English to figure out what those two words meant. We called him a "*culero*" (asshole) in return, and kept playing.

Jorge and Pedro went off to play a game of air hockey. They were daring and bold, and not too smart. Lucas and I were the thinkers. I took charge, since I was the most athletic of the pair. "I'm going outside for a second," I said to Lucas. He was into his game, jostling with the joystick, so he gave me a quick nod. I was hungry. Out on the boardwalk, I saw a crowd gathered around a food court. "Hey, Luis!" I turned toward the voice calling my name. Leticia and Maria, a couple of girls from our class, approached me. They started talking about a ride they'd been on, the Giant Dipper. I was jealous.

Leticia explained how to get on the rides.

"You need to buy passes at a booth first," she said.

She showed me their remaining passes with a proud look on her face. I was cool.

"We're just waiting for the lines to go down," I said to her.

Lucas came out of the arcade and joined us.

"Lucas is scared of the rides," I said to the girls, showing off.

Lucas turned beet red with anger. He heard his name and could tell we were laughing at him. He couldn't do anything. I'd given him plenty of purple and blue marks on his arm at school. Lucas was a regular goof. Plus he didn't speak enough Spanish to make a comeback.

Lucas went off on his own, looking upset. "Lucas, where are you going?" I asked. I lost him in the food court. The girls left and I was alone. My shirt was moist with sweat from playing video games. I hope Leti and Maria didn't leave because I smell, I thought.

I had five, one-dollar bills in my pocket which was all my parents could afford to give me. I noticed a short line at the left of the food lines and kids standing around with chocolate-covered ice cream cones. I went to buy one, believing it'd be easy. I'd just point at the image of the cone pasted on the side of the cart, give the man my money, and grab my delectable reward.

"What'll *ya* have?" the gringo man asked.

I pointed. He prepared a vanilla cone. I handed him a dollar, grabbed the cone, and turned away. I wanted chocolate, but couldn't complain. I had accomplished something new, a purchase in an American theme park. I felt good about myself, licking the cold vanilla cream.

Suddenly I heard a call behind me.

"Hey, kid," the ice cream man said, "you forgot your change."

I got scared. Is he talking to me? I thought. I turned, wondering if I should flee.

"Kid, where are you going?" the gringo asked, pointing at some coins in his hand.

I stood frozen. His language was incomprehensible to me.

"Come get your change!" he said, getting visibly frustrated.

"Me, no," I said, unwilling to complete the broken sentence I had learned, "Me no es-speak inglish," out of fear of sounding alien.

Things got worse. The man saw a security guard pass by his stand. The security guard carried a radio in his hand, wore black khakis, and a grey cotton shirt with the word, SECURITY, in the middle of it. He was a buff black man, thick forearms, with mittens for hands. His swollen biceps stretched out the sleeves of his shirt.

There were two black kids in my class and the man before me was the fourth I'd ever seen in person. There was a black fourth grade teacher at our Elementary school, Mr. Gibbs. Back in December, on the last lunch recess before Christmas vacation, Mr. Gibbs put on Michael Jackson at the MTV Video Music Awards. M.J. had unveiled the moonwalk to the world and danced to "Billy Jean." The hype about Michael Jackson's performance had been so widespread. I don't think I would've accompanied my friends to Mr. Gibbs' class otherwise. He'd been called the meanest teacher at the school and I was scared of him.

If it wasn't for Michael Jackson, his charisma and flare, I think I would've peed on myself. Standing there that day, seeing the ice cream man talking to the black security guard, was one of the most unnerving experiences of my life.

"Can you give this change to that kid there?"

"Sure," the guard said. "Which kid?"

"That one right there," he said, pointing at me.

I shook my head nervously. No, I didn't try to steal that money from the change jar, I thought. Please don't take me.

I'd heard that park Security took you to the police if you did something wrong. The police would whip you with something called a "ticket." I imagined getting lashes with this "ticket." I've been hit in my open palms with a ruler back in Meoqui, but a whip? I asked myself. This is serious.

Even scarier, I'd also heard of kids getting dropped off at the Immigration Office by the police. I didn't want to get deported.

The black man walked toward me, intimidating me. I was going to drop my cone and make a break for it, but my legs wouldn't budge. It was as if my sandals were stuck to the wooden boards below me. Before he got to me, Lucas reached me from the side.

"Here you go, son," the security guard said, holding two quarters in between his index finger and thumb, lowering his tree trunk of an arm toward my caved-in chest. "You forgot your change."

I didn't want the coins. I assumed he was showing me what I'd tried to steal.

"I'll take them to him, mister," Lucas said. "Thanks!"

No Lucas! I said to myself. What are you doing?

The man relinquished the quarters.

"Anytime, kid," he said to Lucas.

The trip back to the Santa Clara valley was faster going downhill. I flipped from daydream to reflection as we descended the mountain. My classmates were laid out along their seats, sleeping, wasted by the park. Mrs. Garcia turned around to look at us like a mother hen. I was wide-awake, and she gave me a big smile. I smirked in return.

I stared outside the window, thinking of Lucas. How he had rescued me from the security guard, the police, and the Immigration. By the time we got back to school, I had decided to never make fun of Lucas again. It was great, being more popular because I was smarter, faster, and stronger. It was entertaining to take advantage of Lucas, speaking in Spanish. Yet he possessed strength none of us (Mexicans) had: The power of English. As I'd learned in Santa Cruz, knowing English is what mattered. Now *I* desired this power, more than anything else.

Karina's Coin Toss

"It's just like a coin toss, child," *el Padre Ramirez* said. Karina listened closely as the Father tried explaining why children turn out bad. "I'm not a gambler of course. That's both a sin and a vice. You know, even God," crossing his forehead in the process, making the bench he sat on creak from the sudden movement, "had to deal with Lucifer." Karina was given prayers to recite before she left Sacred Heart, told to do so below the image of *La Virgen de Guadalupe*, and to go with God.

Karina had grown up in *Los Altos de Jalisco*, the Jalisco Heights, within the semi-dry, mostly flat Arandas municipality. She was of good stock. Her parents, Marcos and Ines Aragon, were dedicated *tequileros*. The family had produced the tequila as a livelihood for three generations, starting with Karina's great-grandfather, Don Francisco. They had horses, the best gamecocks, American trucks, and most of all, they had pride.

The blue agave was good to the family, allowing Karina and many of her siblings to attend the best schools. Karina herself had been sent to the *Colegio Inglés*, a boarding school with an English speaking focus in Guadalajara. Her parents bought her the best church dresses as a child. She liked to wear a black tiara to Mass, to keep her long, blonde hair back. Karina was the type of girl that wouldn't go anywhere without a male escort.

"I've decided to go to U.N.A.M," she said, telling her parents where she'd go to college.

"Great choice," her father said. "You know," he added, "Octavio Paz, Alfonso Robles, and Mario Molina all graduated from there. You could be among them someday."

"*Si, hija,*" her mother said. "A Nobel Laureate in the family is exactly what we need."

"I'm majoring in Law, *mami.*"

"Excellent," her father said businesslike, "we could use a lawyer."

Karina had a top-notch education. Apart from the instruction at the *Colegio*, she had summer tutors and mentors. They molded Karina into an independent and competitive woman. They taught her to question authority. Sunday school was meant to develop Karina into a well-balanced individual. She wouldn't be complete without learning about morality, sin, and temptation.

Karina's parents were proud of their daughter. The schooling they paid for had been worth every *peso*. They'd raised a perfect child, ready to take on the world. As a show of confidence, they gave Karina little advice on the morning of her departure. They were out on the driveway, late summer of '75.

"Do you have everything?" her father asked.

"*Si, papa,*" Karina said, hugging him.

"*Bueno, hija,*" her mother said, "you take care."

"Wish me luck," Karina said, hugging her.

"You won't need it," her father said.

The classes Karina took at the university were tedious and boring. Her professors were respectable, mostly haggard old men with specific erudition. Eventually she met one worth her interest. She met *el Dr. Villalon* at the start of her junior year.

Villalon was different. He was intelligent like the other professors, but he liked discussing his social life during lectures. To spark interest in his students, he told them about drinking and dining with Mexico's top politicos. Karina's ears perked up each time. She'd always imagined having powerful connections and friendships one day. Could the professor open doors for me? she thought.

As the eldest child, Karina believed she had a duty to her family. She needed to keep the Aragon legacy alive. Karina's parents didn't need to tell her this. Their tequila, ARAGON, was built on tradition. Her father's ancestors had started and grown the family business. Her father had acquired a council seat and sponsored the municipal president. As one of the most successful *tequileros* of Arandas, Don Marcos was the epitome of success.

The ambiguous relationship between Villalon and Karina began with a coy smile. Karina sat in the first row. Villalon, the old dog, played bashful. His wrinkled face, brown eyes, and gray hair, made him look harmless. His deep voice was well suited to his profession. At sixty, he was still handsome.

Villalon was Karina's stepping stone. After class she waited patiently for the other students to finish speaking with him. She stood close to him, invading his personal space, pretending to be interested in the class. Villalon, aware of her advances, didn't mind the opportunity to stare at Karina's breasts.

Villalon enjoyed Karina's company. They walked around campus, discussing Mexican politics. "Would you like to accompany me to a party at the governor's mansion?" Villalon asked Karina, during one of their chats. "To celebrate his re-election."

"Really?" she asked, surprised. Finally I hit the jackpot, she thought.

"How do you know the governor?" she asked Villalon on their drive to the party. She wore a red evening dress with black heels, revealing only her petite feet.

"I helped him with his first campaign and provide him with legal counsel," he said, with an aura of importance, complemented by the black suit and red bow tie he wore. He left his car with the valet and gave the man a tip. "Join me," he said flaring out a bent arm, inviting Karina to his side.

The geezer looks cute, Karina thought. "Certainly," she said.

The mob of socialites in attendance blocked view of the beautiful marble floor. The crystal chandelier illuminated multiple white faces in expensive suits and dresses. Karina's first impression was that of an indescribable opulence. There was enough power in the room to rule the entire country. Villalon escorted her to a group of three men.

"Good evening, gentlemen," he said with a smirk.

"Villalon!" one of them said. "How are you old-timer?"

"Extremely fortunate as you can see," he said, glancing at Karina.

Karina blushed, matching the rouge on her cheeks.

"Karina Aragon, these are the *Licenciados* (attorneys), Gustavo Diaz, Franco Miranda, and Jose Paz," Villalon said.

"Pleasure to meet you all," Karina said.

"The pleasure is ours," Miranda said eagerly.

A scheme, that only the men could see, was unfolding.

"How do you know Professor Villalon?" Karina asked.

"We're his former students," Miranda said.

"Of course you are," she said.

"And you are his pupil," Miranda said.

The small talk continued between Miranda and Karina. One at a time the other men excused themselves, starting with Paz, until only Miranda was left. Even Villalon found a way to leave the two together. "Excuse me for a minute, Karina," he said to her. "There's a gentleman here I must speak to."

Miranda charmed Karina. He told her jokes, making her feel comfortable around people of importance. He introduced her to the governor. He gave Karina the starring role in a fairytale.

Before she learned of his accomplishments, Karina considered Miranda's looks average. Miranda was the Institutional Revolutionary Party's (P.R.I.) leading candidate for president. I can totally see myself with him, Karina thought. But she didn't suspect that Miranda, and his associates, were in business with the Professor. That the recruitment of young, attractive, ambitious women for powerful men took place at U.N.A.M never occurred to her. Villalon made it look natural, leaving Karina with Miranda, giving her the opportunity to strike like a snake in ambush. "May I have her back?" he'd asked Miranda with a pretense of urgency.

Miranda and Karina dated for six months. He drove her all over town, behaving like a prince. They spent evenings dancing in discotheques and eating at fancy Cuban restaurants.

"I'm married," Miranda said to Karina, buttoning his shirt with his back turned away.

She lay naked on the bed in a room at the Sheraton Maria Isabel Hotel.

"That's why we've never gone to your house?" Karina asked. "I thought it was all part of your flare for the finer things in life."

"You're not angry?"

"No," she said, "I suspected as much."

"Well, nonetheless," he said, tucking his shirt in, "this is the last time I'll be seeing you."

Karina remained calm.

"Don't you love me more than you love her?" she asked, expecting him to reconsider.

"Actually, I don't," he said. He took his wallet out, placing some money on a night stand. "For your cab," he said, taking one last look at himself in the mirror before leaving.

Karina's visit to P.R.I. headquarters was a desperate attempt to kindle an extinguished fire.

"I'm pregnant," she said to Miranda.

"Foolish girl," he said. "You have the nerve to come to my office and try to pin *me* for your university indecencies!"

Miranda had security kick Karina out of the building. But she was with child, his child.

Karina was humiliated. How will I break the news to my parents? she asked herself. She considered playing the victim, taken advantage of by a crooked politician who'd broken his promises. The scenario wouldn't work. Her father was a proud man. He wouldn't let a dirty politician take his daughter's honor, blemishing the Aragon name. Besides, Miranda was powerful enough to make people disappear.

An abortion went against Karina's catholic upbringing. Her mother would never forgive her for destroying a life. There was no way out. Karina made up a story, and told it to her parents in Arandas. A French student had been responsible. He'd courted Karina with his European looks, his enticing accent, and lured her into transgression. He left Mexico not knowing he'd impregnated his "little Mexican princess."

"You must contact him!" her father demanded. "Surely this man comes from a good family."

Her mother didn't buy it, but wouldn't interfere with Karina's story. Ines' silence frustrated Marcos.

"Ines, you must say something," he said to her. "Convince your daughter to give me this man's name and whereabouts in France."

Ines eventually learned the truth and condemned Karina for being manipulative. Marcos Aragon meanwhile had a delicate situation on his hands. He was a man of great esteem and this was the first scandal the family ever had. There was no way to hide a growing belly. He gave Karina an ultimatum.

"You either tell me who this scoundrel is and where I can find him, or you and your bastard child will have to go!"

"But where to?" she asked, crying.

"I don't care where you go," he said harshly. "Just go far from here. We'll tell everyone you went back to school."

Karina's child was born in January of '77, at the Alexian Brothers Hospital in San Jose, CA. When her father told her to go far away, Karina did just that. She left Mexico to put her past behind. Karina didn't immigrate to San Jose as her countrymen had. She'd traveled by air with a visitor's visa. Her parents knew the right people to buy their daughter a visit to the U.S.

"Where are you planning to stay?" the man asked, back at the American embassy in Guadalajara.

"San Francisco," she said. "We have friends from Arandas there."

"We're giving you a six-month tourist visa," he said, stamping her passport.

But Karina intended to stay permanently.

Settling-in was hard at first. Karina wasn't used to living so cramped. In Arandas, her father's hacienda was several acres from the closest neighbor. Now she lived in an apartment with neighbors directly above and to her right. Her apartment on Alum Rock Avenue was adjacent to a hallway and close to a cement stairway leading to the second floor. A central courtyard with picnic tables and lounge chairs provided the residents with a cool spot on warm San Jose evenings. With her window open she could hear Spanish spoken and occasionally some English. Everyone got along great. It'll be a fine place to raise Diego, Karina thought, eventually liking her new place.

As a two-year-old, Diego was unrelenting and mischievous. He climbed out of his crib, hiding and knocking things over. To give the nanny a break, Karina rented Disney movies, hoping they'd keep Diego occupied. Instead of watching the videos, Diego ejected them from the VCR, placing them in the toilet while the nanny was distracted. Karina didn't worry about the losses. She was doing well financially. Her English speaking abilities helped her get a job, working for ROLM Communications as custodial supervisor. But having to take time off from work to find nannies stressed her out. Several overmatched nannies gave the same excuse to quit:

"Su hijo es pesimo, señora," or "Your son is terrible, madam." I wonder if Franco Miranda behaved like this as a toddler? Karina asked herself. On her side of the family, no child that she knew of had ever behaved like Diego.

By the time he was eight, Diego had logged fifty hours of detention at Mayfair Elementary. Diego's teachers were frustrated. At a parent-teacher conference, they described to Karina how Diego acted in class.

"He can't sit still, won't focus on his work, and he consistently distracts others," the most senior one said. "It's really a challenge for us, Ms. Aragon, focusing all our attention on your son with thirty other kids in the class. This is probably not the best time to tell you this, but we think he stole another kid's lunch money last week."

"Where's your evidence?" she asked.

During a meeting when Diego was eleven, a school counselor made a suggestion: "There are some tests I can conduct to measure his abilities," she told Karina.

"Absolutely not!" Karina said. "My son isn't stupid."

Meanwhile, Diego terrorized the residents at the apartment complex. He recruited other kids to tag along at night, ringing doorbells, playing "ding-dong ditch." Stomping feet, running, and laughing, could be heard in the hallways on most late evenings. He smashed pots in the courtyard, broke lawn furniture, and convinced smaller kids to jump from the stairway rails. Children got hurt. The residents were furious. Several neighbors came knocking on Karina's door one night, giving her attitude. "Maybe you should control your own children!" she said to them, slamming the door.

At James Lick High School, several students reported that Diego was the leader of a group of marijuana dealers. Even with three of the sellers pointing the finger at him, Karina suspected he was being falsely accused. "Did you actually see him handing marijuana out?" she asked the vice principal. "I studied law in Mexico," she said, trying to intimidate him.

"Mom," Diego said, "tell me again about my father."

"He was a powerful attorney," Karina said proudly. I've got to change it up, she thought. Perhaps a tragedy will motivate him to follow in his father's footsteps and get serious about school?

"He would've been President of Mexico one day," she said to him, lying, "if he hadn't died in a car accident before you were born."

"What about my grandparents?" Diego asked.

"They're wealthy *tequileros* in Jalisco, *mijo*. You'll meet them someday. As soon as I get my green card."

"Does that mean I get to drink all the Tequila I want?" he asked.

As an eighteen-year-old, Diego was five-foot-nine inches tall and medium built. He had light-brown hair that he wore spiky like the leaf of the agave. He was ordinary looking, just like his father, with a nose proportional to his face, semi-square jaw, and rigid cheeks. His eyes were hazel like his mother's, and would've given him an innocent stare, if it weren't for one of them being lazy. Co-workers at Shakey's Pizza couldn't tell where he was looking, if his focus was on them or on something else. His voice was assertive and his intelligence seemingly average. He was charming and convincing like his father, and manipulative like his mother.

On the evening of August 4, 1995, a Friday, Karina answered a knock at her apartment door.

"Good evening, madam," a San Jose police officer said, trying to look inside the residence.

Karina stood in between the opened door and door frame, blocking the officer's view.

"Good evening," she said cautiously. "How may I help you officer?"

"There've been some robberies in this complex," he said. "Three of your neighbors had break-ins. The last one happened yesterday between the hours of nine and eleven p.m. They said you have an adult son living here?"

"Yes," Karina said, "my son Diego."

"Right," the officer said, looking at his notepad where he had written Diego's name. "Can I talk to him?"

"He's not here," Karina said, lying. "He told me he was going out with friends from work after their shift. He works at the Shakey's on Story Road."

"I see," the officer said. "Could you tell me where he was yesterday between the hours of nine and eleven?"

"Here with me," she said. "We stayed up watching television until 11:30."

Being Diego's alibi bothered Karina. Have I gone too far this time? she thought. Defending her son was part of her motherly role. But Diego wasn't a minor anymore. A feeling of shame struck her. What have I done? she asked herself. Looking for answers, she drove to Sacred Heart the following morning.

She hadn't been to church in a long time. Still, Father Ramirez received her with open arms.

"I feel like an accomplice," she said to him, confessing she'd covered for Diego.

"Everything will be fine, my child," he said, trying to console her. "Maybe turning him in will make you feel better?"

"I'm afraid, Father," she said.

"Afraid of what, child?"

"Of losing him," she said with her eyes beginning to water. "He's all I have."

Karina drove home after her prayers, contemplating the statements she'd made during confession: Why am I so scared of losing Diego? It doesn't matter. It's not happening!

Diego was home when she arrived.

"What are you getting ready for?" she asked, seeing him in front of the mirror dressed nicely.

"I'm going out with friends," Diego said.

"You're going out?" she asked. She wanted to confront him and mention the officer's visit. She wanted desperately to lash out and order him to stay home. Fear got in her way. "Where to?"

"Just around," he said.

"When are you coming home?"

"I don't know, mom," he said. "Stop asking so many questions."

Karina felt like she'd been kicked in the gut. She was living in a dream, believing she could control Diego. He was a man now.

"I'll leave dinner in the oven," she said.

"Nah, don't bother," he said, leaving the house. "I'll be eating out."

The door slammed shut. Karina was dejected. She'd failed as a daughter, a lover, and a mother. She began to sob with thoughts about Diego racing through her mind. Diego was the reconciliation with her past. Diego was the key to her happiness. He should've lived up to his potential, Karina thought, wiping her tears. He was born of excellent stock. That hadn't mattered. Diego was a screw-up that like many other Mexicans would one day be imprisoned. His making had been a coin toss, a gamble that failed to pay off. There was nothing else for Karina, but to accept her fate.

The Secret

The laws were clear. They weren't going to be changed because of one man's fancy rhetoric or his desperate use of *argumentum ad misericordiam*. Mr. Richardson, clean-shaven, with sparkling blue eyes, and a veteran of many cases, could do nothing except apologize. He couldn't believe the outcome. He thought for sure the panel would've considered the special circumstances, the boy's success. The teen was an example of what could be achieved in the United States with hard work.

"I'm sorry, Mr. Hernandez," Richardson said on his cell phone. "They just didn't see it our way."

"Well," Martin, the boy's father, said. "What now?"

The Hernandez's didn't move to Carlsbad because of the perfect weather or majestic sunsets. Being able to take strolls along the cliffs, watch surfers below, or shop at the Village, hadn't factored into their decision. They settled in the Carlsbad Barrio because it was close to Mexico. Maria Hernandez and her eleven-month-old son, Brayan, had left Tijuana in November of '94, a month after Martin. The two bedroom apartment near Jefferson Elementary marked their beginning, humble like that of most immigrants, but promising.

Maria stayed indoors with Brayan for six months after their arrival, unnerved by the experience she endured crossing the border. She recalled that day and played it out like a movie scene, tormenting herself by inserting a tragic outcome. She hid with her son in a makeshift-hiding place added onto a '94 Ford Bronco.

"Please hurry," Maria said to the Coyote driver, crammed below the cabin with Brayan wedged between her breasts.

Brayan had slept quietly most of the way, but was roused a few vehicles from the inspection booth. The sounds of the border, old engines rattling, impatient drivers honking, the yells of destitute vendors holding up cheap trinkets and food, were at fault.

"Almost there," the Coyote said.

Before the Bronco got to the line, Brayan began crying uncontrollably.

"¡Calle ese niño!" or "Shut that kid up!" the callous man said.

Please, please hurry, Maria said to herself desperately, worried she'd asphyxiate her son. She smothered Brayan's mouth with her chest. The fear of getting caught by Immigration was intense, causing Maria to temporarily lose her mind and put the life of her child at stake. Maria suffered from postpartum depression. Motherly instincts kicked-in after the Coyote's shout, urging her to keep the child alive. Once in U.S. territory, she felt at equilibrium for the first time.

On the day his wife and son left Mexico, Martin had waited nervously in Carlsbad. He'd gone ahead of them to find a place to live. He paced anxiously back and forth at the apartment, biting his nails, wondering if they crossed successfully. The Coyote's phone call came later in the evening, bringing great news.

Thanks to her older brother, Jose, Maria soon got a job at an Oceanside Taco Bell. She'd not heard of a Chalupa or a Burrito Supreme, but she liked how the food tasted. She was petite, standing only five-foot-four inches tall. She put on a few extra pounds and had to wear the Taco Bell polo size medium, due to the added weight. The net she wore to cover her curly brown hair irritated her skin.

Despite initially being uninterested in her son, Maria had come to love Brayan. She understood postpartum depression now, and loving Brayan gave her confidence that she could bond with another infant. Stephanie came two years later, born at Tri-City in Oceanside—an American citizen.

Martin was brave and hard working. He was the voice of the family, a risk-taker, and he made tough decisions. He was passive, but became active when his family needed him to lead. Providing for his family was his number one priority. His beige skin had become bronze from a constant routine of picking avocados, oranges, and tangerines out at the groves in Fallbrook. Like Maria, he believed education was the key to a better life.

Much to his parents' delight, Brayan loved school.

"He's so smart, Mr. and Mrs. Hernandez," Brayan's third grade language teacher said. "His English is better than most of the students in the class."

By 6th grade, Brayan had exited the English Language Development program. By 8th grade, his foreign accent had disappeared. Aside from excelling in the classroom, Brayan was gifted athletically. He'd earned the starting point-guard spot on the basketball team. Making the yearbook as "Most Likely to Succeed," was his most cherished middle school accomplishment.

Brayan wanted to understand the hardships his parents faced before immigrating to the U.S. They told him about Tijuana, the shops on Calle

Revolución, the beaches, the poverty and crime. He tried picturing their stories, but without seeing Tijuana firsthand, he couldn't relate.

"Mom, can I go to Tijuana with Uncle Jose and Aunt Julia this summer?" Brayan asked, prior to starting high school.

Because of their undocumented status, his parents couldn't take him.

"No," his mother said, "your uncle doesn't have room to take you."

Jose was like a bridge for the Hernandez's. "Maria can work at Taco Bell with Julia," Jose said to Martin, encouraging him to cross the border. "I know some people who work as ranch hands in Fallbrook. They may be able to get you a job."

"How am I supposed to know where you're from *if* I don't visit?" Brayan asked his mother.

"You will someday," she said, walking away. "Just not now."

Brayan was close to his Uncle Jose and Aunt Julia. Julia, a white, middle-aged woman, managed the Taco Bell where Brayan's mother worked. Jose, a lanky forty-year-old, was an electrician for San Diego Gas and Electric. Brayan enjoyed spending time with them, listening to his uncle brag about his past, watching his aunt shake her head in response. "Man, you should've seen what a little badass I was in high school," he told Brayan. "The administration at Oceanside didn't know what to do with me."

"Brayan, Stephanie, come here," Maria said, pulling out the family photo album.

"Not the birthday pictures again, mom," Stephanie said, seeing her mother flipping pages. "We don't have time for this right now. School starts tomorrow."

"Is this at Lego Land?" Brayan asked, humoring his mother.

"Yes," Maria said, sighing. "How time flies."

At Carlsbad High School, Brayan thought of himself as a popular teen. He liked to fit in with all of the student groups: the jocks, skaters, surfers, nerds, and anyone who was friendly. His charisma helped him get along with all of his teachers. Though there were other Mexican-American students at Carlsbad, Brayan didn't associate with them. He didn't share anything in common with them. They listened to Latin music, and he preferred hip-hop. They spoke Spanish often, and his was rusty. Mexican boys played soccer at lunch, and he hung out with his teammates instead.

Brayan, five-foot-eleven inches tall, joined the highly ranked water polo team as a tenth grader. He stood out from his white teammates in a Speedo because of his dark brown complexion. His teammates treated him without prejudice. What mattered to them was Brayan's performance in the pool. He was tenacious on defense and kept the Lancers' rivals from scoring.

Brayan wanted to be a credit to Mexican-Americans, not an affirmation of a stereotype. Noticing himself in class amongst a sea of white students motivated him to excel. By the time he was a junior, he'd amassed a 3.7 grade point average in mostly honors and Advanced Placement level courses. By the end of the year, Brayan was in the top 100 students of his graduating class.

"He has to know now," Martin said to his wife.

"No," Maria said, "let's wait a little longer. Just a couple more months."

Martin and Maria wanted to let Brayan know that he, like them, lived in the country illegally.

Throughout the years they'd kept knowledge of his immigration status from him, hoping reform would happen. Their secret came out unintentionally, during the summer prior to Brayan's senior year. Brayan was filling out online college applications in his room.

"What!" Brayan said to his mother. "How's this possible?"

Maria remained silent, noticing her son's face slump.

"All these years and you guys didn't tell me? Why did I try so damn hard then?"

Brayan sat down. His torso hunched like a wilted stem. He stared at the carpet, stunned. He tried looking up, but couldn't. Tears formed in his eyes, and he was too embarrassed to let his mother see him cry. Martin walked in the room, looking for Maria.

"We're sorry son," his mother finally said, beginning to weep. "We wanted you to try in school and do the best you could."

Stephanie joined her family, hearing the commotion from the living room.

"What's wrong?" she asked.

"I'm an illegal and you're not," Brayan said. "*That's*, what's wrong!"

They didn't leave Brayan's room for hours, talking things out, consoling each other.

Senior year was a train wreck. Seeing no point to continue working hard, Brayan became apathetic and his grades dropped. His teachers would ask if he was okay. He'd shrug his shoulders. To his coach's surprise, he quit the water polo team. His teammates objected, pleading with him to stay on the team. Brayan ignored them. Outreach came from a school counselor: "Is Brayan okay, Mr. Hernandez?" Brayan had lost his grandfather whom he dearly loved. That was the first of many excuses his father used to cover for him.

At home, Brayan had a dejected spirit. He was a teen without a mother or father. He became deaf to their cries to stay motivated. To Brayan, Maria and Martin were betrayers, leeches who'd sucked the life out of him. "If only the Dream Act had passed," Maria said to her husband after another day of getting the silent treatment.

Brayan's depression morphed into aggression. He developed a short fuse with his sister. Everything she did annoyed him. "Aren't you going to do anything?" Stephanie asked her parents, frustrated. Brayan had pushed her across the living room. But there was no response from either Martin or Maria.

Jealousy was another manifestation of Brayan's anger. "You don't even have good grades!" he said to Stephanie one evening. School had been the way he'd channeled his energy. With his education in peril, Stephanie's American citizenship had become Brayan's focus. He hated that she was eligible to go to college without restrictions. "But you can still go to college, son," Martin said. "We can afford to pay for you to go to Junior College!" California's AB 540 made it possible for undocumented students to register for junior college, without needing to report to INS. Brayan could even qualify for in-state tuition. But he couldn't proceed past junior college. Without the help of Federal Student Aid, his parents couldn't afford his schooling. Only legal residents and citizens like his sister qualified for federal loans.

The summer after Brayan graduated from high school, Maria was given Immigration advice at Taco

Bell. Carlsbad was full of vacationers. The visiting Mexican-American couple from San Antonio was trying to be helpful. They overheard the conversation Maria was having with a co-worker. The woman, a mother, volunteered a suggestion.

"You should hire an immigration lawyer. I bet they can convince INS to give him a green card...Did you say he's been in the country all his life?"

Maria and Martin met with Mr. Richardson soon after. "Oh yes," he said to them, "I've handled many cases like this. I'm positive I can get Brayan his residency." Mr. Richardson worked from home. The Hernandez's had come across his ad in the North County PennySaver. They wanted their son back. They wanted him to realize his dream and graduate from college. They spent all the money they'd saved on the lawyer. If they'd done a thorough check, instead of taking a leap of faith, they would've discovered a history of poor performance.

"They said we hadn't proved his legal status," Richardson said outside the San Diego Field Offices in his best Spanish, gringo accent.

"What do you mean by 'we,' Richardson," Martin said.

"Sir," Richardson said, "I told them you and Maria live in Tijuana, that Brayan and Stephanie live with their uncle in Carlsbad, and that Stephanie needs her big brother. Just like we had talked about."

"And what about your assurances, sir?" Martin asked. "You told us we had a good chance."

"And you did! They set a deportation date for six months from now—"

"What!" Martin said, becoming pale.

"What did he say?" Maria asked, seeing her husband's reaction.

What have we done? Martin thought. He and
Maria were ruined. They had no money for an
appeal. Now their beloved son was registered with
the INS and scheduled for a deportation. What could
he say to his wife?

"Put Brayan on the phone please, Richardson,"
Martin said. Martin looked at his wife with a calm
expression on his face.

"He doesn't want to speak with you, sir,"
Richardson said. "I tried passing the phone to him
many times."

Martin couldn't blame his son for not wanting to
talk. Brayan wasn't an ungrateful child.

"He told me to tell you something else, sir,"
Richardson said. "He's not coming home. He's going
to go stay with his uncle."

Maria and Martin could put their minds at ease,
knowing they'd tried their best to help Brayan. The
secret they'd kept for many years no longer
consumed them. Brayan would return to Tijuana in
six months, and they'd go with him. Maria and Martin
were grateful that Brayan had received a quality
education. He'd learned to speak English and knew
enough Spanish to get by in Mexico. He wouldn't
have a problem getting a job anywhere in Baja.

Rosarito Beach Hotel several years later:
An American family drags their luggage
through the "Bienvenidos" archway and into the lobby.
Slowing them down on their way to the desk is the
lobby's glamour, colorful Spanish tiles, a large central
stairway, and a glowing chandelier.

"Hello," the woman said, as her husband pulls
bags and two toddlers closer to her.

"How may I help you?" the man at the desk asks.

"Oh," she said, "we have a reservation for four, under Johnson."

The man smiles at the woman, looks at the entire family with a quick glance—a clutter of khaki shorts, beach sandals, and cotton tank tops.

"Will there be anything else I can help you with today, folks?" the man asks, a few keystrokes and a signature later.

"No, I believe were fine," she said. "Thank-you, *Bray-yan*."

"You're welcome," he said, smiling insincerely.

"Well, actually," she said, with an innocent look on her pasty, sun-blocked face, "there is one thing. Where did you learn English? You speak it *so* well."

"It doesn't matter," Brayan said with a look of disgust.

The Debt Collector

David woke slightly early on Monday, November 7th, 1983. It was 6:45 a.m. The light from outside seeped through the blinds, bothering David and causing him to cover up in bed. His first fully wakeful thought was about the day ahead. He was starting a new job, working for a company that specialized in medical bill collections. Not the type of job that made him want to leap out of bed, but it was work. David hadn't worked for three months.

The air in the room was cold. David got out of bed, immediately buckled from the chill, and hugged himself. On his way to the bathroom, he rubbed his arms to get rid of the goose bumps. The thermostat was set to sixty-five degrees. David practiced energy conservation. He couldn't afford to pay Pacific Gas and Electric more than eighty dollars a month.

David relieved himself in the shower. A yellow stream of liquid fell toward the hole of the tub. The tub belonged to the landlord, so David didn't care if it stained or corroded. Seven months ago at the same time, seven a.m., David was showering in his own bathroom. He and his wife owned a three bedroom, two-bath single family home in South San Jose. They'd loved the place. It had carpet in the bedrooms only, and a spacious kitchen with a window to the backyard where they'd see their child playing. Life was great then.

David now had bachelor pad, a place he couldn't really call "home" without his ex-wife and son. Apart from its grimy tub, the one-bedroom studio David rented in Central San Jose had many flaws. The porcelain sink had been badly chipped by previous tenants. A central gas heater was enough to keep the place warm. The kitchen's linoleum floor was white, but he hadn't mopped since he'd moved in. The kitchen cabinet liners were old, cracked and bent, and made a nice hideout for cockroaches. A GE PortaColor television with a metal clothes hanger antenna was the living room's focal point. The tune knob had come off and David needed pliers to change the channel.

Mornings had been David's favorite time of the day. Seeing his six-year-old son, Luke, sitting at the table eating cereal, watching Strawberry Shortcake cartoons, lifted his spirits. David hated his medical telemarketing job, but it put food on the table. Picturing Luke's milk moustache kept him amused at work, while his wife's kiss goodbye gave him the resolve he needed to stay motivated.

Marlene didn't leave David because he was fired. She told him she was leaving him because he'd become a sloth. He stopped fixing broken things around the house. He stopped mowing the lawn, and the garbage piled up. He wasn't responsive to her affections. He'd become complacent at work, and seeking promotions stopped being a priority. If he hadn't been a negligent husband, she would've been David's pillar during his unemployed days. Seeing David's behavior change had taken Marlene by surprise.

David was slim when he first began dating Marlene. He talked about starting his own marketing company in the future. He had drive and great physical features. He was six-foot-two, had dirty blond hair that he kept trimmed, brilliant blue eyes, and manly jaw lines that met at a protruding chin. He wore slacks, a long-sleeve white shirt and tie everyday, though the dress code at work was casual.

He started being lazy a year into their marriage, after Luke was born.

David couldn't explain his lack of energy, why his desire to help Marlene had suddenly dwindled. Am I depressed? he asked himself. She'd call him to set the table, or throw out the garbage, and he'd move with a snail's urgency. "Dave!" she'd yell at him, failing to get his attention. "Sure, honey," he'd say, finally roused from his television trance. The chores wouldn't get done.

Had he not loved Luke so much, Marlene would've left him sooner. She realized he'd been reciting a sales pitch all along: "I promise you'll get what you're asking of me from now on," he told her. "Things will change, I promise." He got twenty pounds heavier in seven years. That's how David changed. Marlene filed for divorce and moved in with her parents, taking Luke. She left David one last task, to sell the house. He sold the home, but not without a struggle. Having to coordinate appointments between him, his wife, and the agent, was extremely difficult for David. He'd show up late, unprepared, forgetting documents he was supposed to have signed. After the sale of the house, David lived off his share of the proceeds. He'd frequent coffee shops and parks, restaurants and bars, until the money ran short.

Fernando didn't need an alarm to wake him. The television noise from the living room each morning, where his son slept, told him it was time to get up. *Fernandito*, little Fernando, was an early riser. He slept on the couch, and got up at 7:00 a.m. to watch Romper Room and Friends on KTVU Channel 2. Without any instruction from his father, he'd serve himself a bowl of cereal. *Fernandito* wished he could be on the show, but knew he'd clam up because his English was poor.

Fernando had taught his son to fend for himself. He didn't have a woman to help him take care of the boy. He had never imagined being a single father. Fernando had been raised by two parents in Delicias, Chihuahua, Mexico. As a young man, he envisioned himself married, having a traditional Mexican wife to handle the children and home. His wife would be loyal and submissive, and address him with respect. In turn, he would provide for her, buy her whatever she needed, and take care of her physical needs. He thought he found his dream girl in Rosanna, a beautiful seventeen-year-old he'd met during *Las Ferias de San Pedro*, the two-week celebration for St. Peter.

Fernando and Rosanna married in 1975. He was twenty, and she was eighteen. In 1976, he and his pregnant wife crossed the Rio Grande and made it onto U.S. soil without difficulty. Friends from El Paso gave them a ride to Gilroy, California, where Fernando and Rosanna had jobs waiting. The garlic factories needed cheap labor at the time.

The young couple resided with friends in Gilroy for two years. The bedroom they rented was adequate at first. They had enough space to move about the room, sit and enjoy each other's company. The birth of their son, *Fernandito*, complicated their living situation. Three people to a bedroom wasn't practical. They saved their money for a deposit and rented their own apartment in East San Jose.

Life in America didn't turn out as Fernando imagined it would. In San Jose, the rent was double what they'd paid in Gilroy. Instead of $300, they had to shell out $600. Plastic diapers, formula, and clothes for *Fernandito* left them little money to buy other essentials. Each Sunday they drove to the Berryessa Flea Market to get groceries and toilet paper. It wasn't the life either of them wanted, but it was better than living destitute in Mexico. To Rosanna's disappointment, she had to find a job after the baby was born. They couldn't afford daycare, so Rosanna worked the night shift at a 24-hour diner.

The hospital bills for *Fernandito's* birth mounted and went unpaid. Fernando worked construction and like everyone in construction, he was at the mercy of the weather, and the consistency of projects. When he worked, the money was good, and they could indulge themselves. A family outing downtown to the Jose Movie Theater was a luxury they enjoyed.

Rosanna wasn't a great mother. Of the few hours a day she had with *Fernandito*, she'd spend less than an hour interacting with him.

"Mom can you help me with my homework?" *Fernandito* asked her multiple times.

"Go ask your father," she'd tell him.

She dragged her feet around the kitchen, making her son bologna sandwiches instead of warm meals. She cooked all night at the diner. Cooking was the last thing on her mind at home. Fernando would get irritated.

"Make him something better to eat," he'd say to her. "He's a growing boy."

He too wanted something good to eat after a hard day's work. She was tired. He was tired.

Trouble between Fernando and Rosanna began when *Fernandito* was four. Instead of her usual two a.m., Rosanna started coming home later, three, sometimes four a.m. The streets are no place for a decent Mexican woman to be late at night, thought Fernando. He interrogated her, waking her up purposely one day to answer for her whereabouts: *"¿Donde chingado estabas anoche?"* or "Where in the fuck were you last night?" She pulled the pillow over her head and told him to go to hell. She eventually admitted going out with friends.

"What friends?" Fernando asked suspiciously.

"Just some friends from work, okay?" she said. "What do you want me to do? I'm locked-up in here all day!"

"How about taking care of your kid?" he asked, screaming.

"Oh," she retorted, "now he's *my* kid. *You* were the one that wanted him."

Fernando and Rosanna argued openly day after day. *Fernandito* would turn the volume knob, putting Romper Room on full blast. They stopped arguing in late August of '83. It was a typical school day morning and *Fernandito* could hear his father moving about the bedroom. Fernando walked out barefoot, with his work pants falling down his emaciated waistline. Fernando wasn't wearing a shirt, as it had been hot all night. The apartment was still steamy. *Fernandito* placed the gallon of milk in the fridge after filling his bowl. *"La piruja de tu mama nos dejo"* or "Your mother the prostitute left us," Fernando said to him.

Fernando woke up on the morning of Monday, November 7th, hung-over. He had spent his entire Sunday at a friend's house, drinking Budweiser. *Fernandito,* and the other boys, had played empty beer-can soccer. Their fathers had stood along a wall, bragging of things they'd done in Mexico, trying to one-up each other. Fernando and the other men pissed outside, aiming their stream at a fence because the woman of the house didn't want drunken men inside.

Fernando got out of bed irritable and nauseated, thirsty for another cold one. He didn't have any beer in the fridge. His throbbing head went unrelieved. He stared into the medicine cabinet mirror and saw a pale face. Unable to recognize himself, he splashed water on his eyes. Fernando was five-foot-eight inches tall. His charcoal black hair was peppered with white along the sides. Before marrying Rosanna, his eyes were pure brown. Now they looked like muddied water. Three weeks of not working had allowed Fernando's face to heal from multiple sunburns.

Fernando left the bedroom in his boxers to check-up on *Fernandito*.

"I want you to pay attention at school, you understand?" Fernando asked. He stood outside the bedroom door like an indomitable tower. *Fernandito* looked up from the kitchen table, quiet and obedient. Fernando grabbed his own chin and stroked his stubble. "I need you to translate later for me," he said, "some bill collectors keep calling about your bitch of a mother."

Fernandito wondered if he'd upset his mother. On his walk to school, he thought that perhaps he'd disappointed her in some way, and that's why she'd left him alone with his father. The fights he'd heard were not always about him. Sometimes they shouted things he couldn't understand. *Fernandito* had one parent left, and now all that mattered to him was not disappointing his father. His dad was ragged without work, thinner without his mom, and less patient with him. *Fernandito* had never pulled his sheet from the couch cushions. He'd always dropped-off his backpack by the door. He used to leave his clothes on the bathroom floor. After his mother left, his habits began to annoy his father. Fernando would snap at him: "You finished the toilet paper and didn't put in a new roll!" and "You didn't throw out the garbage like I asked, you lazy brat!"

Fernandito was six-years-old and in first grade. He'd made considerable progress learning English at school. He was producing simple sentences, still confused, "he" with "she," and vice-versa. The eight stars after his name on the posted class list were evidence of his progress. Having to speak English, especially with adults, still scared him. He felt self-conscious, listening to himself fumble with the language.

David got to work at 7:50 a.m., ten minutes early, trying to make a great first impression. His supervisor was not there yet. He sat upright in a lobby chair until his new boss arrived.

"You must be David," a man wearing a polo shirt said, extending his hand.

"Yes," David said. "I didn't see you come in."

David stood up tall and shook the man's hand firmly.

"Side door," the man said, smiling. "Come," he said, "let me show you your workstation."

David got a proper industry orientation. He got a stack of files and was told he could be firm, but never belligerent with customers. He was told not to use the word "sue," and to avoid getting confrontational, unless in self-defense.

"How does all this work?" David asked his supervisor.

"That's the beauty of it," he said. "You get salary and commission. You get twenty-five percent on anything you collect, the company gets forty, and the referring hospital gets the rest."

David placed the items he'd brought on top of his desk. There was a four-by-six picture of Luke, an electric pencil sharpener, and a couple of pencils. He also pinned two postcards on his cubicle wall: a Lamborghini Countach and a Ferrari Mondial. He drove a 1978 Ford Pinto coupe, and dreamed he'd own either roadster some day. He stood up to look around, and saw several males hunched over, enclosed by their own cubicle. He'd heard from a friend that medical bill collection had lucrative potential.

"There's tons of money to be made," his friend said. "If you can collect."

"How much money?" David asked.

"Depends on you. How badly do you want it? I do need to warn you though, David, it will be hard."

"How much harder can it be, Ron?" David asked. "I've lost my wife, my son, my home, and my job."

David went through his stack of files. He dialed the number. There was no answer. He left a message, reading from the script he'd been given. He dialed another number and got a response. He shuffled the sheets, looking for things to say. The debtor pushed back at every turn. David had to give up on the call. On a third call, a debtor gave David a piece of his mind: "Listen you slimy, worthless, piece of shit, I'm not paying!" the man said. David was proud of himself. He'd kept his cool.

David struggled all morning. He didn't collect a single credit card number, penny for himself, or the company. Lunch gave him a respite from his rookie incompetence. For lunch, David had orange juice, a ham sandwich, and two vanilla wafer cookies. He'd gone grocery shopping at Gemco the day before.

Sunday morning grocery shopping, prior to the ten a.m. NFL football game start, had become routine.

There were other people in the lunchroom, but David wasn't much for conversation. He thought of Luke as he ate, wondering how Luke was doing in school. He thought of Marlene, if she'd found work. Ron and his ex-coworkers flashed through his mind. They used to eat lunch together across the street at a diner. I bet Ron's having his usual tuna melt right about now, he thought. David began feeling nostalgic. The feeling remained in him until his alarm watch started beeping. He had to get back.

David walked to his station. His cubicle neighbor was in the middle of a conversation. David began eavesdropping behind his wall.

"Ma'am," his co-worker said, "if you don't pay us right now our lawyers will sue. No ma'am, we don't care that you don't have any money on you right now. Do you own a credit card? We need a payment right now! You can pay your credit card a month from now."

A half hour later, David purposely walked by another co-worker. He listened-in on his conversation, and heard an aggressive tone. Nobody was following protocol. David didn't agree with breaking the rules like his co-workers' had, but they were effective, collecting from the debtor each time. David grew upbeat. He knew he could do the same and finally make some money. If he made enough money, he could appeal for full custody of Luke. Currently, David could see Luke only on weekends. He looked at his next file. The names, Fernando and Rosanna Mendoza were written on the top. He called the number.

Fernando was having a siesta when he heard the phone ring. The noise was hard to dismiss. The aspirins he'd taken hadn't helped his nausea.

"Bueno," Fernando said.

"Hello, this is David Richards with DebtRecovery. Is Mr. or Mrs. Mendoza in?"

"Mi no espeak inglish," Fernando said. "Yu kal ten minuts?"

"Oh, okay," David said, realizing he'd come across a language barrier.

Fernando hung up and looked at the clock, 1:30 p.m. *Fernandito* was fifteen minutes late. Anger began growing in Fernando like a steam kettle building pressure. *Fernandito* rushed through the front door, huffing and puffing.

"Where in the fuck were you?" Fernando asked. "Didn't I tell you this morning I needed you to translate?"

"My teacher kept the class after school because of some kids," he answered.

"Sure," he said, "blame it on the teacher." He walked by his son and grabbed some envelopes from the kitchen table. "You see these? These are what your goddamn mother left us with, a bunch of bills. I stopped paying when she left. I want you to tell those sons of bitches to stop calling this house. Tell them she doesn't live here and I'm not paying. All we have is fifty dollars to last us the month."

After his father's rant, *Fernandito* turned on the television. He walked to the kitchen and grabbed a bowl. He ate Coco Puffs on the couch while watching cartoons. Later, he pulled his homework from his backpack and worked on it at the kitchen table. At three p.m., the phone rang. Fernando was peeing in the bathroom.

"Get the phone," he yelled. "It's probably them."

"Hello," *Fernandito* said, using his best English.

"Hi," this is David Richards with DebtRecovery, can I speak to your mother or father little guy?" David heard the theme song from He-Man-Masters of the Universe in the background. Luke also liked the show.

"She no espeak English," *Fernandito* said.

"Who, your mother?" David asked.

"No, I mean my father."

"Oh, *he* doesn't speak English you mean?"

"Yes."

"Oh, okay. Is he there?"

"Yes."

"Tell him what I told you," Fernando chimed in, pulling up his zipper as he walked toward the kitchen. *Fernandito* nodded nervously.

"Tell your father he needs to pay his medical bills today," David said firmly.

"My father says she not living here no more."

"Who? Your mother?"

"Yes."

"You tell your father *he* needs to pay. Tell him his name is on the bills too."

"He said your name is on it too," *Fernandito* said to his dad in Spanish.

"Tell him I don't care," Fernando said to his son, trying to stay calm. "Tell him we're divorced."

Fernandito didn't want to say his dad didn't care. It seemed rude to him. He also didn't know how to say "divorced" in English. He began to stall.

"He, he, he says—"

"Listen kid," David said, believing Mr. Mendoza was using his son as a shield, "you tell your dad that either he pays or were suing!" David was in a battle now, his blood pressure rising. The weight of failure hung from his shoulders.

"What did he say?" Fernando interjected impatiently.

"I…I didn't understand him," *Fernandito* said ashamed. He'd never heard the word "sue" before.

"What are you good for then? Tell him we don't have the money and that's that!" his dad said, flicking his hand.

"We no money, he not pay," *Fernandito* said.

David was tired of the loser he'd become. To him, this call represented the line in the sand.

"Tell your dad that either he pays or I'll have Immigration knocking on his door!"

"Papi," *Fernandito* said concerned, *"nos va echar la migra."*

Fernando became possessed. He grabbed at his belt and began sliding it out. He didn't see his son. The boy suddenly reminded him of Rosanna. *Fernandito* had her eyes and nose, and he could see Rosanna in him, now more than ever.

Seeing his father mad, *Fernandito* dropped the phone and left it dangling. He looked to get away, but the room was too small. The kitchen table blocked his escape.

"Hello. Hello." David said, hearing the phone clank.

"Didn't I tell you what to say!" Fernando said, grabbing *Fernandito* violently as he attempted to race by. A loud crack was heard. The belt and buckle struck *Fernandito* on the back of his legs.

"No, *papi*, don't hit me," he said. "I promise to say it better next time!" He shrieked in pain and agony. Crack!

David realized what was happening. What have I done? he thought. He'd pushed a destitute man to the brink. David thought of Luke. He could never hit Luke. He wasn't capable. Marlene had been the one to discipline the child.

"Good for nothing!" Fernando said, slinging the belt harder, punishing the Rosanna in *Fernandito*. Crack! Crack!

"Sir, sir!" David said. "Don't hurt your son!" Before losing the nerve to keep listening, David heard one last plea: *"¡No papi, por favor!"*

David placed the Mendoza file purposely out of sight. On Friday, David reviewed each file before submitting them to his supervisor. The notes he'd written for each would be reviewed. His supervisor would reassign every "still active" file. What am I going to do about the Mendoza file? he thought. He couldn't write, "paid in full" at the top. By the end of the month, the accounting department would know he'd lied. There was only one thing he could do.

The following Monday:

"David, follow me to my office, please," his supervisor said.

David got up from his station and calmly followed his supervisor.

"Shut the door," his supervisor said.

"Yes, sir," David said. David stood in front of his supervisor's desk.

"David, we seem to have a problem."

"What sort of problem, sir?"

"I assigned you ten files last week. You've turned in nine."

"Yes, sir, I did."

"Well, what happened to the tenth file?"

"I misplaced the file, sir. It may be lost."

"I see," his supervisor said. "David, that file is the only record we have of that account."

"I'm sorry, sir. I had no idea."

"David," his supervisor said, shaking his head slowly, "I'll have to let you go unless you find that file by Friday."

"I'll do my best, sir," David said, walking out with his head high.

Challenger

By fifth grade, I had advanced past the idea that swings and slides were the pinnacle of fun. I had fully embraced the more mature sports of basketball, football, and baseball. Basketball was my favorite. At recess, a group of fifth-grade boys ran to the equipment manager and fought over the basketballs. We ignored the red kick balls, leaving them to the younger kids. We abandoned the two-by-two, yellow squares on the blacktop, where we once competed at Four Square. The rectangle of the basketball court was our favorite shape. The competition was fierce. The challengers assembled each morning, looking to dethrone our undefeated squad, "S.J. A-Team." At stake: bragging rights.

Lakers and Celtics games were the best shows on television. I enjoyed watching their games, pretending to be Magic Johnson, even though my game was more like Larry Bird's. My friend Julian and I argued almost daily: "Larry's better because he can shoot," he'd say. I'd defend my favorite player: "Magic can shoot too! He chooses to pass the ball."

Julian was skinny. He had beady brown eyes, a crooked nose, and black hair that he wore flattop style. He liked the Celtics and despised Los Angeles. Julian was born into a powerful culture—the notorious *Norteño* Street gang, the Northern Californian Mexican Mafia. Julian's dad was the shot-caller for *Varrio Horseshoe*. Julian's grandfather had also been in a gang. By the time Julian was three, he'd learned to hate Southern California and anything blue, to love the color red, and the number fourteen. Julian knew Roman numerals before anyone else at school, one number in particular, XIV. He was a natural leader and his leadership transferred onto the court. He was our point-guard.

Julian and I had the same fifth-grade teacher, Mr. Watkins, a clueless middle age white man with a beer belly. Watkins spent the day taking our crap. We tossed wadded papers at him when he wasn't looking and left tacks on his chair. Once, my classmate Thien caught a gopher. Before coming to class, Thien placed the animal in a shoebox. Julian and I dared him to release the rodent under Watkins' desk. Noticing the critter, Watkins screamed like a girl. Julian, Thien, and I kept our laughs subtle. Watkins looked pissed-off. His eyes bulged out and looked like they'd pop from their sockets.

We called Thien our "F.O.B. (Fresh Off the Boat) Asian Assassin." Thien could sink jump shots from another zip code when "on fire." He was born in San Jose. So he really wasn't an F.O.B, or an Asian immigrant. He'd get upset when we called him by his nickname and got even by making Mexican jokes. He got us good right before vacation.

"Why do Mexicans make *tamales* for Christmas?" he asked Julian and me.

After a collective silence, he said, "Because they have nothing else to unwrap."

Thien's parents were from Vietnam, refugees who settled in the Santa Clara Valley. Thien was smart, working out the math dittos faster than anyone in our class. He and I both struggled in Language. English was new for us both. He was the shortest player in our squad, only four-foot-seven. He had long brown hair, black eyes, and a small nose with flared nostrils.

There were few white kids at our school. My class was blessed to have the two best white athletes in Mark and Blake. I'd recruited Mark to be part of our team. I nicknamed my token white friend after a Laker, "Rambis." Julian had recruited Blake, nicknaming him after a Celtic player, "McHale." The twins played like their namesakes. Mark hustled all over the court, diving for loose balls. Blake grabbed rebounds and was a genius on the post.

Mark and Blake were our squad's alleged ringers. Teams claimed Mark and Blake came from South San Jose to play for us. "Mark and Blake are too poor to be from the South Side!" Thien would say, whenever our team's legitimacy was questioned. We hated being called cheaters. Mark and Blake would stay quiet, bobbing their heads in unison agreeing with us. The brothers lived in a trailer park close to school. Their father had left them, and their mother was on welfare.

I don't know how Mark and Blake weren't smelly, wearing the same clothes every day. Mark wore a faded black AC/DC shirt with brown corduroy pants, and black Coasters from Payless Shoes. Blake wore blue Levi jeans ripped at both knees, a faded black Metallica shirt with a hole under the right armpit, and Coasters as well. Every time Blake took a shot, we'd see his underarm. Their outfits helped my teammates and I tell them apart. Mark and Blake stood five-foot-four, had blond hair, and were freckled.

I was third tallest on the team and fast, able to outrun everyone during fast breaks. I never got winded which was great for our offense. My mother said my endurance came from being one-quarter Tarahumara Indian. She said I'd inherited large lungs from my grandfather. My mother and father came from Chihuahua, Mexico. They talked constantly about the Sierra Madre and Copper Canyon, telling me they'd take me there one day. My folks were proud Mexicans. All my life, to no avail, I'd tried to understand their pride. They listened to *musica Norteña* and *corridos* or ballads. The accordion, guitar, and sixth bass were their favorite instruments. I preferred the drumbeats of Run DMC and the Beastie Boys.

My parents and I moved to San Jose from El Paso, Texas in '81. I was five at the time. I remember my summers in Texas. I'd be stuck inside my apartment all day. The air-conditioner would be blasting. I'd let the chilled air hit my face and not pull back until my eyes felt dry. In San Jose, we lived in a duplex and our place was shaded by trees. The summer heat in San Jose was pleasant compared to El Paso. A cool bay breeze was the Santa Clara Valley's air-conditioner.

The morning of Monday, January 27th, 1986 was cold. The temperature had dipped below freezing overnight. There was frost on the roofs and lawns. The frost made me reminisce about grass skiing with my friends. We couldn't afford skiing so we slid across our school's field. I'd do a partial front squat, arms reaching forward, and lean back. Two of my friends would hold me up, one to each arm, and they'd pull me full-speed until their strength gave out. My shoes and socks were soaked by the end, but I didn't care.

Since the morning was cold, I'd put on my black-hooded sweater. The heat from the early sun left me feeling toasty. Whitewashed jeans were in style. I wore the only whitewashed pants in my wardrobe. Knockoff sneakers completed my attire. I saw Julian coming off Lincoln Street, walking with his usual strut like Shaggy from Scooby Doo. He wore gray Dickies, black Nike Cortez's, and a Forty-Niners sweater.

"Who do you think will challenge us today, Manny?" he asked, joining me across the street at the light on Willow Road.

"Probably those kids from Mitchell's class," I said. "What did they call themselves?"

"The Knight Riders," Julian said softly, staring at the ground. "What a bunch of posers."

Julian wasn't his usual talkative and cheery self. We walked in silence, hands in our pockets, until we almost reached the school. A patrol car passed by and the officer stared at us.

"He's probably making sure *us* ghetto kids don't cause problems." Julian said. "Fucking pigs. They locked up my old man again last night."

I shook my head with false disgust, providing Julian with false sympathy as well. I didn't like gangsters. My parents told me they were lowlifes, terrorizing neighborhoods. Someday, Julian and I won't be allowed to hang out. He'll get pressured by older gang-members, *La familia,* to help claim territory, and forget school. My parents will pressure me to achieve the American Dream.

Watkins looked disorganized as usual.

"I forgot the dittos in the copy room, kids," he said, walking toward the door. "I'll be right back."

"Watkins you suck!" Thien said.

Everybody laughed. We talked and hung-out until Watkins ran through the door, hugging papers to his belly. Flustered, Watkins started yapping about space ships and the moon. He became excited, talking about a launch happening the next day. He said there was a teacher astronaut going on the voyage.

I didn't care about spaceships or teachers. From the looks of my friends, Julian yawning, Thien falling asleep, Mark and Blake's blank stares, they didn't care either. On my mind was the game, how I'd fare against the Knight Riders. A kid named Juan was on the Knight Riders' team. Juan was fast, but tired quickly. I'll be running circles around him, I thought. I looked back at my friends. Julian was slouched on his chair with arms crossed. His eyes were fixed on his shoes. Blake and Mark looked pale and weak, sitting at the back. I'd seen them practically inhale their breakfast earlier. I wonder if they're still hungry, I thought. Thien was zonked out.

Our behavior was on autopilot inside the cafeteria. We waited in line every day holding our trays. Once we got to the counter, we swiped our ticket then got our food. On Mondays we got hamburger and tater-tots. Tuesday was pizza. On Wednesday we ate burritos. I skipped lunch on "Mystery Meat Thursday." I went back on "Lasagna Friday." I'd heard a rumor that President Reagan called ketchup a vegetable. To get my daily vegetable portion, I'd drown my hamburger and tots, pizza, and burritos with ketchup.

My friends and I devoured our hamburgers and tots. This was my second free meal of the day, same for Mark and Blake. Thien and Julian had to pay forty-cents. It was called, "reduced lunch." After we ate, we left the cafeteria. As reigning champions, we took our sweet time walking to the court. The Knight Riders were already there, warming-up. It was futile and a wasted effort on their part. Thien began trash talking. He teased the guy with the ball, "Pass me the ball, Punky Brewster," he said. "Let me show you how to shoot." We almost wet our pants, doubling over in laughter. We weren't worried about the Knight Riders. We should have been.

The game started inconsequentially for both teams, a bucket a piece on our first possessions.

Julian brought the ball up for our second possession. He made a careless high pass to a wide-open Thien on the corner. The ball sailed past Thien's reach. The challengers capitalized on our mistake. The Knight Riders' point-guard saw a streaking Juan. Juan raced by me and caught a smooth bounce pass for an easy lay-up. We were down a bucket.

"Alright," said Julian, "let's go S.J. A-Team!"

Julian tried to get the ball to Blake down in the paint. With perfect timing, the Knight Riders' defender used his superior strength to front Blake, stealing the incoming pass. The challengers went off on a fast break. Thien's complaint to Julian left them behind on the play, leaving the rest of S.J. A-Team short on defense. The Knight Riders' point-guard lobbed the ball inside to a forward, beating Mark to a position underneath the basket. They scored again, and now we were down two buckets.

I set a screen and released Thien from his defender, but Julian's pass was late and Thien's shot was swatted. "You got packed, Thien!" an onlooker said. Thien gave him the bird, running back on defense. I got back quickly and stole a pass to Juan, lobbing it to Julian crosscourt. Julian went up for an easy lay-up. The ball came off the side of the rim. He missed. "What the fuck!" he screamed.

The Knight Riders grabbed the rebound and attacked, pressing forward. We'd lost our composure. Their guard got the ball on the left wing. He shot from about twenty-five feet. We were sure he'd miss. The range was too far for anyone on their team. S.J. A-Team set up for the rebound, but the shot went in. Everything was going against us. Our frustration peaked, and we disintegrated on the court, insulting each other, forgetting the teamwork that'd made us a difficult team to beat. We made one final run and got to within two baskets, but it was too late. The lunch bell rang.

Mark, Blake, Julian, Thien, and I didn't talk the rest of the day. Watkins couldn't figure out why we were quiet. Since we didn't interrupt, Watkins continued talking about the Tuesday space launch.

Old Watkins was excited the morning of Tuesday, January 28th, 1986.

"Kids," Watkins said after the Pledge of Allegiance, "talk to your neighbors while I set up the television."

"That's *gonna* take you all day, Watkins!" Thien said.

Watkins ignored Thien and kept working. I looked at Julian.

"Shouldn't have called you a 'ball-hog' yesterday," I said to Julian.

"I deserved it," he said. "I wasn't focused."

"Your dad?"

"Yeah, man," he said, looking down. "I know he's a bad dude, but he's still my *jefecito* (old man), you know."

Some of us had wandered off. Watkins asked us to get back to our seats. He turned the channel to the station broadcasting the launch.

"It's almost time boys and girls," he said, raising the volume. "That's the shuttle at the Kennedy Space Center."

"We can read you know!" Thien said.

"Those are the rockets sticking out in the back," Watkins said. He was trying hard to get the class excited.

The defeat from the day before was on my mind. The television voice grabbed my attention. "T-minus twenty-one seconds...T-minus fifteen seconds…T-minus ten…," the announcer said, before crackling radio transmissions interrupted him. "Ten second countdown, kids," Watkins screamed, keeping us quiet. The announcer's voice came in clear again: "Nine, eight, seven, six, we have main engine start, four, three, two, one, and lift-off."

The close-up showed the rockets blasting off, pushing the arrangement of shuttle and metal into the sky, defeating the force of gravity. It was fantastic. A light show like I'd never seen before. Another close-up gave us a good look at the shuttle. It lay atop the main rocket. We couldn't take our eyes off the television. The event confirmed America's greatness. For a moment, I felt loyalty to my parents and their Mexico sink in my heart.

"Velocity 2,257 feet per second!" Watkins said.

"Is that fast?" some lame girl named, Norma, asked.

The television announcer was calm and methodical, giving the listeners a scientific description of the flight. He used some words we didn't understand, "nautical miles," and "throttle." There was a pause. Then something happened, an explosion. Screams from the spectators in the stands on-site made my heart race. Clouds of white smoke filled the screen. A plume made its way further into the heavens before splitting in two. The plume on the right streaked in red, falling back to earth like a meteorite. "Looks like a couple of the, uh, solid rocket boosters, uh, blew away from the side of the shuttle in an explosion," the announcer said. My classmates and I stared at the screen, stunned.

The faces of people watching Challenger's end haunted me that night. Close-ups of distraught family members, and friends of the crew, kept me up. I felt frightened and sad for a couple of days. At school the next day, I felt odd. Gone was the pressure to fit in. I wasn't focusing on how different I was from Thien, Mark and Blake, Julian, and old Watkins. A feeling of solidarity, of mutual grief, had spread throughout the school. The principal of our school made an announcement over the intercom: "Children, today we will need each other the most...your teachers and counselors are also here if..."

Watkins looked like a person in mourning. The girls in my class looked scared. At recess, S.J. A-Team huddled on the blacktop. We hadn't huddled since our first game as a team. We talked about the loss against the Knight Riders and what'd made us fail on the court. We talked about Challenger and the mood at school. We broke our huddle determined and motivated once again. Watkins, the girls, and our school needed S.J. A-Team's best.

Society branded kids like Thien, Mark and Blake, Julian, and me with slurs. We were the sons of boat people, poor white trash, gang-bangers, and illegals. Even though society underestimated us, we rallied like any other American. S.J. A-Team behaved in Watkins' class, consoled second and third graders, and ran errands for teachers. We did whatever we could to help. For the moment, everything was harmonious. For the moment, we showed that we *too* could be counted on.

The Project

"Hey, Bob," Charles said. "How was your weekend?"

Bob was preparing a hydrochloric acid solution at a counter.

"Back-breaking," he said, looking up.

"Really?" Charles asked. "What were you doing?"

"Some yard work," Bob said.

"Honey-do?"

"Yeah," Charles said, "I let the yard get out of control."

"Should've hired a Mexican," Charles said casually.

"What are you talking about?" Bob asked. He put a stopper in the flask and leaned against the counter. Charles walked to a couch in the lounge, carrying a bag and his coffee.

"*You* know," Charles said, placing his bag on the floor, "one of those guys on the corner. I hire them all the time."

"Isn't that illegal?"

"Who knows," he said. "Hiring cheap labor is your right as an American. Why should we pay a premium for help around our homes? Heck, I hired two to build a retaining wall. They did a damn good job."

Bob was twenty-four when he started teaching. It was 1998, and he'd graduated with a science teaching credential. Science teachers were in short supply. At a fair, an East Side Union High School District recruiter offered Bob a job on the spot. Bob's college friend shared that San Jose's East Side Union was great for anyone wanting a challenge. "There's lots of diversity, and you'll probably be placed at a struggling school." Bob wasn't familiar with San Jose's neighborhoods. He grew up in predominantly white Redwood City and had attended affluent prep schools.

The 2001 dot-com bubble burst didn't affect Bob. He hadn't invested in stocks. Veteran teachers at Silver Creek High, where he worked, would nag him. "You need to buy!" one said. "You're guaranteed huge returns in this market," another said. Bob's father, Bob Sr., told him to not follow the herd. "Save your money and wait," he said. Bob admired his father's understanding of finances. He followed his father's advice.

Bob's father was a retired commercial fisherman. Watching his father embark at Fishermen's Wharf was one of Bob's fondest childhood memories. He and his mother waved goodbye from the pier as the Lovely Daisy, his father's ship, sailed off. Then he and his mother, Daisy, would walk holding hands, fighting the cold wind heading for a restaurant. A bowl of clam chowder warmed them before their drive to Redwood City.

Bob was fortunate not having to move from his home as a child. He'd lived in his parent's three-bedroom, two-bath custom Cedar Log home most of his life. He'd see his father on top of the roof, tools dangling from his belt. He'd help his dad clear leaves from the gutters. If his dad wasn't inside, Bob was sure to find him in the garage. "Your home is your greatest asset," Bob Sr. said to Bob.

Bob wanted to be a homeowner. The dot-com bubble burst had made it easier to buy. Were it not for the pink slip he received, he'd have made an offer on his first home. The layoffs were no surprise to Bob. Union reps talked to him about the district's budget shortfall.

"The district tells us that California is in crisis," a union steward said during a lunch meeting. "We'll make sure they keep as many teachers as they can afford."

"Has anything like this ever happened?" Bob asked.

"No," the steward said bluntly.

Bob was two years into his career. Up to then, frequent blackouts were the only sign of California's woes. Bob became disenchanted with San Jose. Home prices skyrocketed, yet demand remained high. "Get in now while interest rates are low," a colleague said to him. The buying frenzy was hard to ignore.

Bob was re-hired at East Side. The chopping block would be there the following year. He worked without job security, hoping he'd survive past his second year and gain tenure. With tenure, he stood a better chance of staying permanently. That year, 2003, had been monumental for Bob. He made tenure status, but most importantly he met his future wife. Brenda was a slender Filipina. She had black hair and eyes, and a light-brown complexion.

Brenda impressed Bob at the annual summer district training. She was at his table, and he couldn't keep his eyes off her. Brenda had engaged three Latino teachers in a conversation about boxing.

"Manny Pacquiao is the best boxer, pound for pound," Brenda said.

"You're out of your mind, Brenda," one of them said. "Mexican boxers dominate every weight class below middleweight."

Bob liked how Brenda stood her ground. He wasn't much of a boxing fan. He preferred to follow baseball. As Brenda defended her idol, Bob imagined the two of them at the Coliseum, watching an Oakland A's game. He asked her out, and a month later, his daydream of catching an A's game with her came true.

"I thought baseball was boring on television," Brenda said. "It's even more of a snore without commentators."

"I'm sorry," Bob said, feeling awkward. "I thought you would enjoy coming."

"Oh, no," she said apologetically. "I'm having fun because I'm here with you."

Brenda taught history at Yerba Buena High. Unable to afford buying a home, she lived in an apartment. Bob was the first white man she'd ever dated. She liked tall, dark, and handsome men and Bob was tall, handsome, but not dark. She didn't mind that he wasn't dark. He was a teacher like her, and he could relate to her professionally. She also liked that he was a regular guy.

Bob's parents were law-abiding and tolerant people. They hadn't talked much with Bob about marriage, or the type of girl he should bring home. "All that matters is your happiness, son," his dad said. They saw Bob brimming with joy the day he brought Brenda over. She'd made lumpia for them, Filipino spring rolls.

Bob and Brenda married in August of 2004. The wedding was held at the Mission Church on the grounds of Bob's Alma matter, Santa Clara University. Brenda's family, the Santos', drove from San Diego. They'd met Bob only once in April, during the engaged couple's spring break. Bob enjoyed his vacation in San Diego. "It's so laid back here," he said to Brenda. "It's like we're in a different state."

"This is ridiculous," Brenda said to Bob.

"I know," he said, "it is ridiculous. How can they pink slip teachers with ten years experience?"

It was 2005. California's budget was billions of dollars in the red. Bob and Brenda lived in Brenda's apartment, saving whatever money they could each month. Two teacher's salaries weren't enough. They'd saved for a down payment for a home, but prices kept surging every month. A subprime home loan was their only alternative. Bob's dad had objected.

"These variable interest loans are awful," he said. "Keep saving."

"We appreciate your advice, Mr. Anderson," Brenda said. "I'm tired of living in an apartment. The neighbors are lousy. There are kids always running around making noise. I don't have enough kitchen space. I can't take it anymore!"

"I told you, Dad," Bob said. "She's made up her mind."

"Sir," Brenda said, "Bob and I aren't going to be left out. We've done everything right. My mom told me, 'go to college, find a good job, marry a nice man, and buy a house.' "

"Can't argue with that I guess," Bob's dad said.

Bob, like Brenda, wanted to be a homeowner. They agreed that a sub-prime loan wasn't in their best interest. However, they were priced out of the Bay Area. After extensive searching, only condominiums were in their range. A condo wouldn't be much of a step-up from an apartment. Moving to a more affordable place was their only option. To be closer to Brenda's family, and to purchase a bigger home, they moved to San Diego County.

"Only $485,000.0 for a three bedroom, two bath home in Oceanside!" Brenda said.

"That's incredible," Bob said. "With a huge backyard and a garage."

"Looks like you can start buying tools, honey," Brenda said.

"Sure," he said sarcastically. "I'm a real do-it-yourself guy."

Brenda's new kitchen had granite countertops, a pantry, and plenty of cabinet space. Best of all, they weren't wall to wall with their neighbors. They qualified for a traditional thirty-year loan. Their Vista Unified teacher salaries paid for the monthly $2,500 mortgage. After car payments, food, and bills, the two had little left over for leisure.

"Can you believe this housing mess?" Brenda asked.

"Actually I can," Bob said.

It was 2006. The housing bubble crisis was in full swing. Their home had lost half its value. There was also mention of an impending economic depression. Some of Bob and Brenda's neighbors stopped paying their mortgages. Bob and Brenda thought about doing the same. They hadn't lost their jobs, but had endured two years of salary reductions. They had made changes, moving to Oceanside to buy their dream home. Now they were expecting their first child.

"I don't care if we're underwater," Brenda said. "I'm not willing to give up our home. We have a baby on the way."

"What should we do?" Bob asked.

"I don't know. But it wouldn't be fair to our child."

After the birth of their son, Brenda and Bob worked additional duties at school. Bob coached baseball, receiving a measly stipend. Brenda became a department chair. The two saw less of each other. They saw less of their son, Michael. The couple struggled, but got by.

In 2008 the banking crisis occurred, bringing with it more worries for Bob and Brenda. To stay afloat, they used coupons and skipped dining out. They drove slower to conserve gas and stopped their cable service. By 2009 they'd paid off their cars and credit cards. By 2010 they were able to start a college saving plan for Michael.

Bob and Brenda hadn't made a single home improvement. The kitchen floor was an eyesore, appalling Brenda each time she cooked.

"I'm done with this floor," she said to Bob.

"What's wrong with it?" he asked.

"Look at it! The grout's worn out, and the tiles have *freakin* faded. Plus it's ugly. We need a new floor, Bob."

"Whoa, whoa, whoa," Bob said. "You know what new flooring will cost us?"

"I don't care," she said.

Bob thought about their financial situation. All these years of holding back, reserving cash for emergencies, for what?

He surprised Brenda, telling her they were going to Home Depot. They were going to check out tile. There were plenty of reasonably priced tiles at the store, porcelain as low as $2.50 a square foot. They chose a cheaper ceramic tile instead.

"$3,000," the Home Depot worker said. "That's material, delivery, removal of your old floor, and installation."

"We'll have to think about it," Bob said, seeing Brenda's disappointed look.

They shopped the project around, getting similar quotes from other installers. Bob told Brenda what Charles had said to him about hiring day laborers. She'd seen Charles before at district trainings, getting into arguments with administrators. Charles, in her estimation, was a loose canon.

"Charles said he uses day laborers all the time," Bob said.

"Go ahead and talk to Charles," Brenda said.

Bob was shocked. Brenda had always told him that Charles was a troublemaker.

"Wow," he said, "you must really want this new floor."

"So how do you go about it?" Bob asked Charles, being purposely vague in case someone walked in.

The two of them were alone in the science staff lounge. Bob had waited until Jenny, one of the other science teachers, left.

"What's that?" Charles asked.

"Hiring a day laborer," Bob said.

"Oh, that! There's nothing to it. Haven't you seen them around? Check Home Depot or near a nursery."

"Yeah, but do you just tell them to get in or what?"

"Yeah," he said, "just tell them what you need and how many of them you want. You take them to your place and watch them work...maybe throw in some sandwiches and water, pay them, take them back. It's simple. What's going on?"

"Brenda wants a new kitchen floor," Bob said embarrassed. "I've never installed anything in my life. Can you believe it?"

"You?" he asked. "Yeah I can believe it."

The two of them laughed.

"You know what to get?" Charles asked.

"Not a clue," Bob said.

"I have most of the tools," Charles said. "I'll make you a list of the stuff you'll need. You can rent a tile cutter at the Home Depot."

Charles told Bob he'd need two day laborers for his project. He could pay them $10 an hour. Bob left school on Friday with a trunk full of Charles' tools.

There were a few items Bob needed to buy off Charles' list. He got up early the following morning. He drove through early morning fog on the 76, heading east toward Bonsall. The Home Depot opened at 6:00 a.m. Bob was anxious. He thought about his father. Would he approve of Bob's hiring day laborers? Bob felt torn. It was his job to deal with the house, not Brenda's. His dad had made homeownership look so easy.

There were several Latino men waiting near the nursery. Bob took the items he'd bought, some rags, a level, and pliers, to his trunk. He looked at the men. They stood around waiting, some with arms crossed, others with hands in their pockets. Bob walked toward them holding a sample tile. He looked both ways like he was crossing a street.

"Speak English?" he asked them.

"Ah lito," a dark one said, stepping forward.

"You know how to lay tile?" Bob asked, pointing at the tile.

"*O, si,*" the man said. "Bery easy."

"Good," Bob said. "Know anyone else?"

"Yes, *mi amigo*," he said, waving at another man.

"Okay, you two come with me," Bob said.

Bob drove off with two passengers. Both sat in the back. Should I make small talk? he thought.

"What are your names?" he asked.

"Juan, and *mi amigo*, Jose," Juan said.

"Nice to meet you," Bob said. "Listen," he said, "is ten dollars an hour okay?"

"Diez bolas la hora, compadre. ¿Te parece bien?" Juan asked his friend. Jose nodded. "Yes, ten okay," Juan said.

The trio didn't speak the rest of the drive.

Bob let the men in his home. Brenda and Michael were in the living room watching television. The men moved in and out of the kitchen all day. They cut the tile in the garage. They removed the old tile. They applied the setting material, installing the new tiles perfectly level. They looked like professionals. Bob was impressed.

The men completed the project in seven hours. Bob handed each man their cash.

"Where should I drop you off?" Bob asked the men.

"Jom Dipo is ohkey," Juan said.

Bob had boxes of tile left over. He placed them in the back of his car, and drove the laborers back to the store.

Bob was feeling good. The day laborers had turned out to be good hands. They hadn't been intrusive or offensive, as Bob had feared. He had worried, imagining the workers stealing from his home. I can't believe I fell for the stereotypes, he thought. Juan and Jose had behaved like professionals. They were respectful, and had been thankful for the sandwich and water Bob had given them. They'd even cleaned up the mess.

Bob noticed a patrol cruiser on his tail. He looked at the speedometer. He wasn't speeding. He looked back again, noticing a green band on the vehicle. It was the Border Patrol. Should I tell these guys to get down? he thought. That would be too obvious.

"Tell your friend to stay still," Bob said. "I have *La Migra* behind me."

"Ohkey," Juan said. "I have papers, but my friend, he no has."

Juan turned his head, facing Jose. *"Quedate quieto,"* Juan said to him.

Bob felt relieved, pulling into the Home Depot parking lot. The INS cruiser had kept going. The agent had pulled up on Bob's left, taken a look at him, and sped away. The moment had rattled Bob.

"That was close, huh?" Bob asked, turning off the car.

"Si," Juan said.

The two men walked away from Bob, talking and laughing. Bob looked at them in awe. They look so content, he said to himself. The entire project had cost Bob a total of $1500. He still had some boxes to return.

Bob walked across the lot, thinking of a happy wife waiting at home. As he neared the automatic doors, a strange feeling engulfed him. Bob turned to his right and saw a man staring at him. The man wore a scarlet cap. He wasn't certain, but the emblem on the man's cap looked to be military. Bob entered the store feeling uncomfortable. He walked quickly toward the returns register and got in line.

"You know," a voice said moments later, "you shouldn't be hiring illegals."

Bob turned around. He saw the man that'd stared at him a few minutes before. The man had followed him inside. Bob read what was on the cap, Retired Vietnam Vet: Semper Fi. Taking a closer look, Bob saw that the man had a white beard, was heavyset, and had on black shorts. Out of respect, he refrained from saying anything to the man.

"It's un-American," the man said.

Bob became self-conscious. The people in line appeared to be judging him with their eyes. Bob ignored the man again. Hurry up, please! he thought, looking at the woman behind the register. Finally it was his turn. He had his exchange processed and headed quickly for the exit.

The following Monday, Charles asked Bob how the project turned out. Bob told him what happened at Home Depot.

"It's kind of funny, isn't it?" Charles asked. "The government uses propaganda to keep middle-class citizens from getting ahead. We're told not to hire people who may be in the country illegally. So what happens? Our costs go up. Meanwhile, they give big companies tax breaks and allow jobs to go overseas."

"I felt guilty," Bob said pensively. "I still do."

"Nah, man," Charles said, "don't feel guilty. You're doing your part for the economy. Who cares where money flows, so long as it keeps moving? I *betcha* those illegals are going to Wal-Mart with your money."

"That old Vet shamed me," Bob said.

"You should've told him to mind his business!" Charles said. "He's probably sitting cozy in retirement with a nice military pension. *He* doesn't know your situation. You're just trying to look out for your family."

"I know," Bob said, staring into space.

"Damn right," Charles said with a mischievous smile.

Ascensión

During offertory, Ramon saw his old friend Daniel stand up and take a basket. He took his eyes off Daniel and faced the front of the church, staring at the Christ. He began to reminisce of the time he and Daniel played by the stream. Look at him now, he said to himself, glancing at Daniel again. What a waste. Daniel stepped to Ramon's row. He gave Ramon a faint acknowledgement, nodding and looking briefly into Ramon's eyes.

Ascensión, Chihuahua sits on top of a hill. It's the oldest town in the municipality. Residents are accustomed to snowy mornings in the winter and high winds in the summer. Daniel and Ramon played together along the town stream as children. They enjoyed lifting rocks in search of anything animate. Sometimes they caught small frogs and crayfish. Daniel examined their anatomies and observed their behaviors with keen interest. Ramon was cruel to the animals.

"Daniel, watch this," Ramon said, tearing off the claws of a crayfish.

"You shouldn't do that," Daniel said. "Father Holguin said that all living things deserve respect."

Ramon began to laugh. He set the hapless crustacean on a small boulder.

"Father Holguin *es un pinche joto*," he said. "They're just dumb animals." He stomped on the crayfish, spreading yellow mush along the top of the rock. Excrement and cracked exoskeleton remained on the bottom of his shoe.

"Well," Daniel said, shaking his head in disgust, "I guess you're my best dumb animal, Ramon. Come on, let's go."

Daily life around town was slow during the nineteen-eighties. As kids, Daniel and Ramon spent most of their free time outdoors. Their parents didn't worry that they stayed out until dark. Ascensión was a safe and tight-knit community. As teenagers during the nineties, Daniel and Ramon felt the town's pace quickening. Greed, and the temptation to get rich quick, polluted the air. The talk of the town was a new type of business. In nearby Ciudad Juarez, young men could earn good money and respect working for drug lords. With enough courage and bravado, grown men could become underworld kings. To Daniel, the business of drug trafficking was a house of cards, giving his *pueblo* false hope.

"They say the *gringos* are in on it, Daniel," Ramon said. "It's a sure thing."

"I don't care who's in on it. It doesn't make it right."

They walked along a side boulevard. The music at Pedro's cantina blasted *corridos,* or ballads.

"You hear that, Daniel? That's that new badass song by Chalino Sanchez. In California, they call Chalino a *valiente.*"

"Yeah," Daniel said, "I heard Chalino got into a shoot-out at a nightclub in some place called Coachella."

The sounds of the *corrido* had changed. Accordion and guitar melodies used to be gentle, complementing lyrics depicting bravery and suffering. Now the melodies were loud and upbeat, with lyrics about ordinary men becoming rich and powerful as drug smugglers.

Daniel and Ramon stopped at the corner of the school. It was summer and the school was empty. Ramon leaned back on a wall. "I hear that *La Sierra Tarahumara* is good for growing weed," Ramon said. Cannabis was being cultivated in the Sierra Madre. Drug lords had built their empires in hidden canyons within the ancestral homeland of the Raramuri. "I want to get paid and come back decked out with a wad of dollars in my pocket, just like those other bastards," he said.

Like Ramon, Daniel felt tempted. He too wanted to be someone important and have enough money to burn. What could Daniel do with his patrimony, a small shoe store along the main road? His dad worked and worked, repairing boot heels. He'd see his dad on a stool every day gently swinging a hammer, small nails sticking out from his pursed lips. Daniel didn't want to be like his father, but honor and loyalty coursed through his veins. He turned sixteen in 1993. I don't know what to do, he thought, walking to school. Should I go with Ramon? He saw Ramon jump on the back of an older teen's truck en route to the Sierra Madre.

"You coming?" Ramon asked, seeing Daniel.

"I can't," he said.

"Why?"

"My old man says I have to finish school," he said.

"School!" Ramon said, and began to laugh. "That's a waste of time."

Daniel was held back by a certainty that God would know where he was. Whether he was under a canopy of pines, or driving along the Copper Canyon, or in the sky waiting to land on a clandestine strip, God would judge his every move.

It was a cold winter day in late February when Daniel saw his friend again. An overnight low had sprinkled the town with snow. Nine months had passed. Daniel was on his way to school, carrying a backpack, wearing jeans, a baseball cap, hooded sweater, and tennis shoes. He saw Ramon splashing water on the windshield of a 1994 Chevrolet Silverado. Ramon's boyish face had aged. He had bags under his eyes and was growing a beard.

"Ramon?" Daniel asked from the sidewalk.

"Daniel!" Ramon said, putting the bucket down. "How are you, *primo*?"

"Great," Daniel said, admiring the truck. "When did you get back?"

"A couple days ago. I was going to come by, but I had to take care of some things."

"It's okay," Daniel said, checking out his friend's clothes. Ramon wore a black leather jacket over a brown Wrangler long-sleeve shirt, collar flared. His shirt was tucked neatly into his Levi jeans.

"You like the clothes, *primo*?" Ramon asked.

"*Te ves chingón* (You look badass), but what's with calling me, *primo*?"

"Don't get out much do you? Everyone's a cousin nowadays. It's good gesture and sounds better than *amigo*. Get it?"

"Yeah, I get it, *primo*. And this truck?"

"Oh," Ramon said, "the company vehicle you mean. Come look."

The two talked inside, catching up. Ramon inquired about the town.

"Has anyone new moved to Ascensión? How about suspicious travelers stopping on their way to Juarez?"

Daniel wondered why Ramon asked him these questions.

"Ascensión will be mine one day," Ramon said.

He wants to set-up shop here, Daniel thought. His friends' declaration made Daniel uncomfortable. The town belonged to everyone as their birthright. Unless Daniel was willing to hand himself over to Ramon, be one of his underlings, he had to cut ties with him.

When Ramon came back in town, Daniel was an eighteen-year-old newlywed. In 1995 he'd married his high school sweetheart. Karla was sweet, dimpled, and humble. From the plaza ice cream shop, Daniel saw Ramon talking to municipal police officers across the street. He recognized Lieutenant Hernandez. Ramon was behind the steering wheel of a parked truck. There were three other men inside, one riding shotgun, and two in the back cabin. Daniel handed an ice cream cone, two scoops, vanilla and pecan, to Karla. He heard laughter coming from the truck. Ramon's left arm hung outside the driver's window. The glare from his gold watch blinded Daniel, but the laugh had given him away. Ramon guffawed loudly, then chuckled, just like he used to as a child.

In 1996 Karla gave birth to a baby girl, Diana. The couple was busy, dedicating most of their time to raising their child. Eight years passed. Ramon had slipped to the back of Daniel's mind. Karla, Diana, and his father's aging health were his primary concerns.

When Diana was nine, she was allowed to walk to school alone. Ciudad Juarez was the drug war battlefield, not Ascensión. On a hot morning in late September of 2005, Diana turned a street corner and stumbled upon a dead man's body. The corpse was facing up with guts spewed from its abdomen. A small stray dog was licking the wet, red pavement. Daniel and Karla found out the hard way that the violence had spread.

"Mom, are the bad men going to kill me?" Diana asked.

"No, mija," Karla said. "The bad men don't kill little girls."

"But I found the dead man."

Daniel had regretted his decision to let Diana walk alone. He'd seen Ramon several days before, eating at a restaurant with Hermilio Chavez, an up-and-coming politician, and *el Comandante* Hernandez, the former lieutenant. Ramon's payroll runs deep, Daniel thought at the time.

Diana as a teen was tall, had green eyes, long brown hair, and the body of a model. She'd been the queen of the annual municipal fair at thirteen. She earned excellent marks in her first two years of high school. Daniel and Karla were proud of her accomplishments. Although his daughter had proved responsible, he was waiting until her fifteenth birthday to let her date. *Quinceañera* celebrations marked a girl's transition into womanhood.

"Ramon's house is huge," Karla said to her husband.

Ramon's house had the best views in town, a panoramic view of the desert valley below. It came gated. A sentry checked vehicles before letting them inside the complex.

"Built on a foundation of blood and sin," Daniel said.

As regional lieutenant for the Juarez cartel, Ramon could afford to splurge. His mansion had marble floors, ten bedrooms, and a movie room with theater seating for ten. He had a lighted pool with an eight person Jacuzzi, and an imported crystal chandelier hung in his reception hall. The church too had been expanded and modernized. The town's population had increased from ten to twenty thousand in a decade. The church's prosperity, however, wasn't because Father Holguin's congregation had grown. Envelopes full of American cash were delivered every month to Holguin, courtesy of Ramon.

Daniel at thirty-three looked scrawny and tired. He stood five-foot-nine, and his eyes were constantly blood shot. Glaucoma ran in his family. He had an undersized, caved-in nose, and a thin moustache above thick lips. Daniel volunteered as an usher, collecting the alms for the Father. Diana and Karla always sat in the first row on the right wing of the church. The first row in the center of the church was reserved for the town's most generous resident, Ramon Bernal.

Having to see Ramon during Mass bothered Daniel. Why couldn't Ramon consult the Father in secrecy and leave the church unspoiled? From his pulpit, Father Holguin endorsed the use of drug sale profits for the church's benefit: "All contributions are purified by God's church," he said. Daniel saw Ramon smirking in response. Moments later he caught Ramon staring at Diana.

"Ramon was looking at Diana," Daniel said to Karla at home.

"He's never seen her before, Daniel," she said, slipping her heels off. "Maybe he's curious?"

"He's curious about what's under Diana's clothes," he said, taking off his boots. It had been sixteen years since Daniel and Ramon last talked. He wondered if Ramon had thought of him. They were friends once, and he'd loved Ramon like a brother.

After his father's death, Daniel managed the shoe repair shop. He had to sell specialty boots, and move the business into retail in order to stay afloat. He and Karla were there every day, working long hours. Daniel would never be rich. *"Puro jalar y jalar,"* or "Just work and more work," Daniel's dad said to him as a kid, describing life as an adult.

He and Karla had tried to have another child. Prayers, a blessing from the Father, a regimen of medication, teas and herbs from the town's medicine woman, did not help them get pregnant again. They were disappointed, but eventually got over their inability to conceive believing Diana had been a single miracle of God.

At Diana's graduation party, Ramon and Diana had their first encounter. Daniel had rented a hall for the occasion. The hall was sparsely decorated: purple plastic table covers, small vases with carnations, and *"¡Felicitaciones Diana!"* on a banner made from white butcher paper.

"You should've asked me, *primo*," Ramon said. "I would have helped you make more of this event."

Partygoers began whispering to each other, seeing Ramon speaking with Daniel. Tension began to rise and merriment turned into nervous energy. In Ciudad Juarez a week before, there had been a shooting at a graduation party. Tens of innocent bystanders had been riddled with AK bullets. Diana's celebration came to a halt.

"Please, Ramon, let's step outside," Daniel said. Ramon handed Daniel a bottle of *Sotol*, the Tequila of Chihuahua. *"Gracias,"* Daniel said timidly, grabbing the bottle. Ramon moved slowly toward Diana carrying a bouquet of two dozen red roses.

"For you, *señorita*," Ramon said.

"Don't take them," Karla said to Diana. Diana looked at her dad. Daniel stood frozen. "You can leave them on the table if you like," Karla said to Ramon.

Much to the relief of friends and family, Ramon and his men walked outside with Daniel.

"No," Daniel said to Ramon, "absolutely not. You're twice her age!"

Ramon smiled, checking his men from moving forward with a slight nod. "You should ask *her* what she thinks," he said, getting into his 2011 Escalade.

Daniel bit his tongue.

Diana was a restless seventeen-year-old. Beauty pageants and school no longer interested her.

"Are you going out tonight, princess?" Daniel asked.

"Dad, please stop calling me, 'princess,'" she said casually. "My girlfriends are picking me up later."

Daniel and Karla could do no more than bless her forehead and pray for her safe return. They wouldn't sleep until the door bolt creaked again. Diana eventually broke the news to her father that she'd been seeing Ramon.

"Are you crazy?" Daniel asked Diana. "This man's a killer, a known Mafioso. Do you not see this?"

"I love him," Diana said with a dreamy look.

"Love," he said. "What do you know about love? You're just a child!"

"I'm a woman, Dad," she said. "A grown woman!"

"I prohibit you from seeing him again, and that's that!"

Diana wasn't allowed to go out at night anymore. News of her restriction reached Ramon.

The town was small, but not devoid of technology. With her cell phone and Internet connection, Diana could stay in communication with Ramon.

"Live with me," he said to her after a month apart.

"Okay," she said.

"I'm sending my men."

"Now?" she asked. She didn't think Ramon would act so soon. It was the middle of the night. A neighbors' dog began barking at the sound of large engine blocks nearing the house. Daniel and Karla were scared by the loud knocking at their front door.

"We are here for Diana, *señor*," the lead henchmen said. "Orders from Ramon Bernal."

"What?" Daniel asked. "No you're not."

"Sir," he said calmly but assertively, "orders are orders. Best if you just let her come along."

Daniel saw Karla from the corner of his eye. She looked frightened. The thought of a struggle, of manly bravery he'd only daydreamed about, flashed through his mind. Cowardice and better judgment prevailed. The fight's not fair, he thought.

"Bring Diana," he said softly to Karla.

"But Daniel?" she asked.

"Do it, Karla, please."

"Can she at least pack some things?" she asked, revealing herself to the faces outside the door.

"Everything will be provided, ma'am," the point man said.

Diana had grown up so fast. The loose shirt Diana wore couldn't hide the shape of two voluptuous breasts. She walked out of the house wearing shorts, showcasing her beautiful legs.

"I didn't sentence her to death," Daniel said to his wife after the men left with his daughter. "She'll be fine with Ramon."

"You can't be serious," she said, walking away from him.

Daniel surprised Ramon, showing up at his gate a week later. The walk to the mansion had been nerve-racking for Daniel. Daniel wanted to restore what he'd lost, honor and respect. "There goes *el sin cojones*," a man across the street said to another man. Daniel ignored them and sped up his pace.

A guard patted Daniel down. Daniel was led across the courtyard by the guard and his leashed Doberman. The courtyard was Spanish style with a terracotta tile patio. A mesquite provided sparse shade along the walls to the left of the front entrance. Geraniums and succulents in large clay pots added color. However, Daniel's mind was on his objective:

"You will marry her," he said to Ramon with a racing heart.

"Well, well, well," Ramon said. "I think I like this Daniel better than the old one."

"You can kill me right here, right now. I will not leave until you agree to marry Diana," he said.

A decrepit Father Holguin conducted the wedding ceremony. The Rite of Marriage provided suspense for the bride's invited guests:

"...Ramon and Diana, have you come here freely and without reservation to give yourselves to each other in marriage?"

Daniel and Karla squeezed each other's hand. They wanted to declare that the wedding had been forced. That Ramon had not given them a choice. Everyone remained silent. "We have," Ramon said.

At the end of the ceremony it was all smiles, hugs, and handshakes.

"The three of us are alive," Daniel said to Karla driving home. "That's what matters. Besides, the marriage won't last and Diana will be home with us in due time."

"Why do you say that?" she asked.

"They'll come for him."

"Who?"

"The military."

"*Yeah, I'm sure* the military will come for him," she said.

An End and a Beginning

Two sweaty men, employees of the La Paz Funeral Home of Saucillo, struggled to lower Miguel's casket. The temperature was 110 degrees Fahrenheit. *"¡Porque, porque!"* Bertha, Miguel's mother, said. She leaned her head on her sister's left shoulder, crying in disbelief. "Why so much violence, *Dios mío*?" Bertha asked. The men began to fill the grave with their shovels. The sounds of the shovels striking a dirt mound announced the burial's end. "Evildoers!" Bertha said.

Miguel wasn't smart. He left school in seventh grade and worked as a ranch hand in *La Cruz* municipality. He milked cows, fed pigs, and cleaned the stables. He gave most of the money he made to his mother. After two years, Miguel grew tired of the ranch. He couldn't take the smell of animal feces any longer. The gnats and flies circling his head annoyed him daily. At fourteen, he went to the general store along the main highway and convinced Mr. Ramirez to give him a job.

"I can sweep, stock supplies, whatever you need," Miguel said.

"You and everyone else," Mr. Ramirez said.

"*C'mon*, Mr. Ramirez. I'm better than everyone else."

"Look, Miguel. I don't need help at the store, but I could use a hand at the ice shop."

In the state of Chihuahua, people always need ice. There's lot's of *Carta Blanca* beer to be kept cold on Saturdays and Sundays. Miguel was handy with an ice pick, chipping in half the large blocks for customers. He was okay with a clamp as well, lifting the heavy blocks easily into people's coolers. Sometimes he'd get a cold *Carta Blanca* tossed to him as a tip. When not at work, Miguel hung out with his friend, Chuy.

"I'm buying a white Stetson hat with the money I save," he told Chuy.

Chuy, a dopey, fair-skinned teen called, "the Mennonite," because of his blond hair and blue eyes, thought Miguel was crazy.

"You have three little brothers and a mother to feed," he said. "You have no business buying fine hats, even though you need one, darkie."

Chuy's family lived next door to Miguel's. They ran a small *tienda* or shop from a stand at the corner of their street. Their homes were identical, part of a planned community development. Chuy's family, however, was better off than Miguel's. Chuy had a 42-inch HD television with satellite service. His father had bought a GE microwave and a new Whirpool refrigerator for the kitchen. Miguel's television was analog with three working channels. His mom heated food on the stove, and their refrigerator had recently been repaired for the fourth time.

"We do a little business on the side," Chuy said to Miguel, smoking a joint.

The two stood under a small tree near the town's basketball courts. "That's why I can afford to share this fine *mota* (weed) with you."

No wonder they can afford so many luxuries, Miguel thought. There's hardly anyone at their shop.

Miguel's father deserted him and his mother. Miguel's grandfather died from a heart attack at forty-one. Without a father, Miguel lacked a male role model and guidance. Without a grandfather, Miguel never learned to respect the past, his *cultura*

Chihuahuense. He knew nothing of Pancho Villa or why Chihuahua is known as "The Revolution's Cradle." He was accustomed to his town always being in transition. Families from central or southern Mexico moved in and out, using Saucillo like a truck-stop on their way north. To live in a more stable environment, many of the locals moved to the large cities. Then there were the ex-residents of Saucillo, returning home as a result of being deported from the U.S. Some had been repatriated from Los Angeles, Chicago, as far as New York City. They looked like thugs with their bald heads, with their arms and chests tattooed.

"I've got a connection in Chihuahua City," Chuy said to Miguel, smoking another joint. "They call themselves 'The Rebels.' They put in work for the Juarez cartel."
"Who do you know?" Miguel asked.
"Some *vato*," he said. "They call him, *El Ronco* (The Hoarse One)."
Miguel laughed.
"They say he's got a bad cough," Chuy added. "Smokes a lot."

Miguel and Chuy's dead bodies were discovered steps from the Cathedral. They had been bound with brown packing tape. Their heads were missing. The bludgeoned heads were found outside the entrance to a national monument. *"Por la patria,"* read a crumbled note left at the scene, with a happy face drawn on the page.
"They found Chuy and Miguel, *Doña* Bertha!" Don Ignacio, Chuy's father, said. "My brother in Chihuahua City said they're at the morgue."

112

Chuy and Miguel had been missing for four days. The local authorities had warned Ignacio and Bertha to prepare for the worse. That there were actual bodies to recover had been unexpected news.

"How did your brother know they'd be at the morgue?" she asked with a sad voice.

"He read a blurb in the newspaper."

"What did the newspaper say?" she asked.

He lied. "My brother didn't say," he said.

The newspaper had read:

> The decapitated heads of two young males, each approximately eighteen years of age, one with blond hair, blue eyes, the other with brown hair, black eyes, and a small birthmark behind the right ear lobe were found near...Details of their deaths are still being investigated.

As she didn't own a vehicle, Ignacio invited Bertha to accompany him to Chihuahua City.

"This violence is terrible, Don Ignacio," she said. "Our own children victims of these cowardly scoundrels, these inhuman beasts who've taken over our state."

Ignacio nodded with his eyes fixed on the road.

"Things have gotten so bad," she said, "even in our own little pueblos. Did you hear?"—she paused, looking at him in vain. Ignacio stared at the road— "The Federal Police arrested *Doña* Lencha's son in Camargo. I couldn't believe it. Not little, Jaime. You remember what a nice kid he used to be?"

The morgue was horrific. An old man in a white lab coat, with a badge that read, Martin, showed Bertha and Ignacio the bodies. The room was small, cold, and sterile. Bertha was glad Ignacio was with her. His presence gave her courage. This was the second time the two of them had stared at death. She was with Ignacio when her best friend, Teresa, Ignacio's wife, took her last breath, dying of breast cancer at thirty-five.

"They were tortured," Martin said. "This one, identified as Miguel," he said, seeing the woman cover her mouth at the sight of the face, "had his penis removed, his right index finger cut off, and several ribs broken before they shot him. His death was the better of the two."

"*Dios mío,*" Bertha said, beginning to gag. Miguel's face was almost unrecognizable.

"This other one died from blood loss as a result of the trauma," Martin said, pulling a spare mask from his lab coat pocket and handing it to Bertha.

"What trauma?" Ignacio asked.

"They decapitated him while still alive. There was severe damage to the muscles of his neck, suggesting they were tense at the time. The handy-work of drug cartels."

"No," she said. "Why would the cartels kill our boys?"

Martin shrugged his shoulders.

Were it not for Ignacio, Bertha couldn't have afforded the funeral services. Without Ignacio's money, Miguel's head wouldn't have been sewn onto its body.

"I'll buy the best caskets for both Chuy and Miguel," he said to her. "Miguel was like a son to me as well."

"Thank you," she said looking at him with eyes full of gratitude.

He stared at her remaining male children as they watched cartoons. Don't worry, he thought. You'll pay me back soon enough.

Bertha and Ignacio waited three days, grieving after the funerals before driving to Chihuahua City to meet with the homicide investigator.

"Chuy and Miguel were drug dealers," the assigned investigator said. "They sold heroin and marijuana at the central plaza."

"That's impossible," Bertha said. "Tell him, Don Ignacio. Tell him our sons were good boys."

"That's right, sir," he said feebly. "Our sons would never fall in with the lowlife you have in your city. The boys came here for honest work. My brother, Chuy's uncle, owns a used furniture store here. He needed help at his warehouse, repairs you see."

"Really," the investigator said, "where is this warehouse?"

"Oh," he said. "Uh, you know I don't have the address on me."

"I see," the investigator said with a blank stare. "From the note the *sicarios* (hitmen) left at the scene, your boys worked for a gang with ties to the Juarez Cartel. Here in the capital we have several drug gangs, most with ties to Juarez. We also have rival gangs with ties to the Gulf and Sinaloa Cartels."

"Forgive me, sir, but you're wrong," she said, her eyes beginning to swell. "You have it all wrong!"

"I'm afraid not, *señora*," he said.

"Any leads on the murderers?" Ignacio asked.

"No," he said. "They're probably long gone."

"Lies!" she said, losing her patience. "You tell us lies so you don't have to do your job. Meanwhile the killers run around gloating. My Miguel was a good boy." Tears began falling down the sides of her face.

"*Calma, calma,*" Ignacio said, patting her knee, "the investigator is merely speculating,"—he gave her a moment to wipe her tears and changed his patting to soft repetitive strokes—"there's no proof here."

"Did they send home large sums of money?" the investigator asked.

"What?" Bertha asked, taken aback by the question.

Chihuahua has some of the best roads in the country. Federal Highway 45 connects Ciudad Juarez with Chihuahua City and the rest of Mexico. If possible, Mexican nationals heading south from El Paso avoid driving through the murder capital of the world, Ciudad Juarez. Ironically, there are billboards along Highway 45 that read, "*¡Bienvenidos Paisanos!*"

Bertha and Ignacio headed south on the 45. The sun was setting, casting wide ocotillo and yucca shadows along the road. The fine sand reflected brown and red hues like a Martian landscape.

"Beautiful sunset isn't it?" Ignacio asked, trying to take her mind off things.

"Oh, Don Ignacio," she said. "How can you think of such things at a time like this?"

"Please, call me, Ignacio," he said.

The air conditioner of the 2009 Ford-150 pushed cool air through the vents. They sat quietly and in contemplation. Bertha broke the silence by occasionally whimpering, sniffling, or offering a rhetorical comment:

"The nerve of that man to insist that our children were drug dealers," she said. She thought about the money Miguel sent her every week. Could it have been earned from the dirty trade? The money had been regular in its arrival, something she hadn't expected. Yet her son was an able young man. "You

116

don't think it's true, do you Ignacio? Was Chuy
sending you money?"

"Don't let what that useless official said sway
your opinion of your son. The boys were not
involved."

"It's just that, why else would they have been
killed like that, so barbarously?"

"Chihuahua City is our second largest. The
place is filled with criminal entities. We shouldn't
have let them go there to begin with."

"You're right." She turned slowly away from
him. "It's my fault Miguel is dead." She started crying
again.

"There, there," he said gently taking her hand,
offering an end and a beginning with his gesture.

Los Malandros

Cesar's evening had gone really well. There was a wad of pesos in his pocket. Many new customers had come to *his* spot: the alley behind Lazaro's Cantina on Vicente Guerrero Boulevard. To celebrate, he pulled out a funnel tube and lighter from his pant pocket, and placed a small brown crystal on a piece of foil.

By the time Cesar entered the rehabilitation center, his temporary residence, he was floating on several hits of Mexican mud. The place was poorly lit. An old table lamp, its switch set on low, was meant to provide a safe welcome to the residents. As extra precaution, each night the attending counselor moved furniture out of the hallway in case residents came home intoxicated.

Cesar walked down the hallway feeling like he could walk through walls. As he neared the staff room, he felt the need to take deeper breaths. Not remembering who was on duty, Carmen or Felipe, he staggered toward his room. He'd felt great, but now a dull pain pulled on his chest from inside. Like the end of a movie scene, his eyes began fading to black, until there was total darkness.

Cesar opened his eyes the following day. Where am I? he asked himself, feeling nauseous. Throbbing pain was coming from his head. He touched where his head hurt. A piece of gauze was taped along the side of his forehead. He recognized the room, the faint-colored walls painted with diluted yellow paint. He sat up on the bed, trying to figure out what happened. His pants were on the floor by his tennis shoes and dirty socks. He stared at them, wondering. When he realized their importance, he jumped out of bed and grabbed them, going for the pockets first, pulling them frantically inside out. Empty.

"Hey, hey, who's here right now?" he asked loudly. Pepe, a chubby kid of about ten years of age with skin the color of chocolate, ran in the room.

"You alright, Cesar?" he asked. *"¿Que pasa?"*

"They stole my money and my *chiva, chingado.*"

"I don't know about any money, but your drug stuff is with Carmen. You know they're not allowed."

Cesar got out of bed slowly. His muscles ached as he slid his legs through the leg holes of his pants. He picked up his shirt from the ground, shook it for scorpions and dust, and put it on. His socks were dank. He smelled them. Their foul odor caused him to quickly turn his face away. Dressed, he walked out of the bedroom and down the hallway. Three young men sat in the living room watching the soccer match between Pumas and America.

El títere (Puppet) munched on a straw, sitting with his chest to backrest on a chair. *El búho* (Owl) sat on a giant wooden spool, flicking the ear lobe of *el Gringo*, who wasn't a gringo, but looked so white he could pass for an American. One of these assholes must have taken my money, Cesar thought. As former El Paso gang-bangers and junkies, Puppet, Owl, and Gringo weren't afraid to search people. They would know where to look for cash, where to find hidden contraband. Out on the street the three would've taken everything from Cesar, his tennis shoes, pants, even his shirt. Since they couldn't easily hide clothing at the center, they'd cut Cesar a break and settled for the drugs and his money.

"You got my *chiva*?" Cesar asked Carmen, looking inside the room that had been converted to an office. Carmen, an obese, olive-tanned twenty-year-old, looked up from behind the monitor of a ten-year-old Gateway desktop. She stared at him incredulously.

"How about a 'thank-you' to go with that attitude?"

"What?" he asked irritably.

"You almost died last night, Cesar. You overdosed on street heroin."

"What about the money? It was taken out of my pockets, damn it. I had four thousand pesos when I got here."

"Aren't you listening? The doctor had to administer two doses of naloxone to keep you breathing through the night…said you would have died for sure if you had injected the crap."

Cesar was unmoved.

"When the doctor and I went through your pockets, all we found was your pipe."

"It's not a pipe. It's a funnel tube."

"Whatever…here," she said, pulling the tube out of the top desk drawer, disappointed he'd used again after a month sober. "Get rid of it."

"Fucking bunch of thieves," he said, snatching the tube from her corpulent hand.

"Pepe stayed by you the whole night. You're his favorite you know!"

I don't care, he thought. I didn't ask him to. He hadn't asked to be saved from death either. At twenty Cesar figured he'd lived long enough, longer than he had expected. Every day now was like finding money in the pocket of an old coat, a surprise. He enjoyed living on the edge. High on drugs he felt alive, powerful, and unaffected by pain or struggle.

Cesar was slim, and his skin complexion was the color of vanilla. Hyper wasn't a temporary condition. It was who he was, always on the move. He had a one-inch scar below his right ear, an injury he sustained from a knife fight at sixteen. After the fight everyone Cesar knew began calling him, "Scarface."

Cesar was smart. "There's no limit to what you can accomplish, *mijo*," his mother said to him on his thirteenth birthday. She died from a crack overdose the following day. After his mother's passing, all that mattered to Cesar was surviving alone in the world. The streets of Juarez were tough. For protection and the brotherly love he desired, Cesar joined a gang of other street thugs, other *malandros* like him. Glue, mescaline, alcohol, marijuana, heroin, tobacco, he did it all accompanied by his homies, in the bitter winter cold as flakes of snow fell from the sky white as cocaine, in the dry summer heat with chapped lips, broken skin, and little volcanoes on his forearms.

"Where's my money, *putos*?" Cesar asked Puppet, Owl, and Gringo.

They looked at Cesar with indifference.

"What money?" Puppet asked. Owl and Gringo stayed quiet, allowing Puppet to speak for them.

"*La feria* you stole from me, *cabrón*."

"We ain't got your *feria*," Puppet said with eyes twisted like a crazy *vato*.

"Guys," Pepe said, stepping in, "there's no fighting allowed."

Cesar looked at Pepe thankful he'd intervened. The three to one odds didn't favor Cesar. He left the living room red-faced, and walked outside to the patio. He heard laughing as he walked away. I can't let those guys laugh at me, he thought. Should I go back and confront them? Cesar decided he'd be better off smoking a cigarette.

In 2008 when Pepe was seven, his dad, Rafael, bought a house in a middle-class Juarez neighborhood. Rafael converted the home to an installation for the addicted and their visiting family members, and named it, *Nueva Vida*. He had been involved in the venture at first, but found a good set of counselors could manage the site. He allowed Pepe to hang around *Nueva Vida*. For patients with children, Pepe served as motivation for them to get sober. Pepe also provided much needed levity and unwavering support.

Cesar's cigarette smoke didn't offend Pepe in the least. At *Nueva Vida* patients and visitors smoked freely, so Pepe was used to the smell of burning tobacco.

"What do you want?" Cesar asked.

"Whatcha up to?" Pepe asked.

"Smoking a cigarette. Can't you see, *chingado*?"

"I'm glad you didn't die," he said, sitting on a metal chair, one of the chairs that were used for group sessions in the evenings. It was the beginning of summer in Ciudad Juarez. The temperature was around ninety degrees. Corrugated metal sheets, on top of wooden columns and parallel beams, protected the patio from the oppressive rays of the sun. "I would've missed you."

"Why?" Cesar asked. It was the first time anyone had said that to him.

"You're smart. You fixed Carmen's computer. Got rid of all those viruses. Plus I like that you say '*chingado*' all the time."

"You like that, you little *chingado*?" Cesar asked, flicking the cigarette butt across the patio toward the dirt backyard.

Pepe fell to the floor and grabbed his gut, laughing hysterically at Cesar's witty response. Cesar, hardcore as he was, couldn't help cracking a smile.

Cesar hated personal counseling sessions with Felipe. Because Carmen was a woman, he ignored and was often rude to her. Felipe was a *macho* like him, and he didn't take Cesar's shit.

"Fifteen minutes outside is all you get," Felipe said to Cesar, during their one-on-one time.

"That's bullshit! That's barely enough time for me to go across the street and back."

"If you don't like it—"

"I know," Cesar said, cutting him off, "I can leave for good." He got up upset from his chair and walked quickly toward the door.

"Group session is in twenty minutes!"

Cesar headed for his shared room with a full head of steam. I don't need this place, he said to himself, beginning to gather his things. Roberto, a forty-year-old man, sat upright on his own bed, smoking a cigarette, and reading the newspaper. The room was shared by four patients. Roberto was the resident veteran, "the most experienced of all," he told the others one day on account of all of the mistakes he'd made in his life.

"You don't want to do that," he said.

"Do what?" Cesar asked abruptly.

"Leave this place."

"Who asked you?" Cesar asked, looking around the room, struggling to gather his things. "Just give me a cigarette and keep your mouth shut, old man."

"Sorry," Roberto said smirking, "this is my last one."

Cesar pulled a gym bag from underneath his bed. He placed all of his items in the bag and stormed out of the room, needing a cigarette (laced with heroin preferably) really bad.

"I'm out of this dump," he said, taking one final look, seeing Roberto bury his head in the newspaper.

"Cesar, where ya going?" Pepe asked, catching a glimpse of Cesar heading out to the street.

"None of your business you little *chingado*," he said, stepping outside. The sun's glare temporarily blinded him. He stopped, allowing his eyes to adjust. Pepe caught up.

"You're not leaving us, are you?" Pepe asked.

"What gave it away?" he asked sarcastically. "The bag?" He paced back and forth in front of the house.

"You look like the fire ants I poke with sticks," Pepe said out-loud.

Pepe had witnessed the suffering of many patients during their withdrawal bouts. He knew the symptoms. "*¡Tranquilízate, Cesar!* (Calm yourself, Cesar!)," he said, but his plea came too late.

Cesar bent over, hacking, grabbing his convulsing stomach. A projectile of vomit came out of his mouth. After dry heaving a couple of times, Cesar stood-up, hands behind his neck like a criminal about to be arrested, and took a deep breath.

"You alright?" Pepe asked.

"You ask some pretty stupid questions sometimes," Cesar said, wiping his mouth with the bottom of his T-shirt.

"Yeah, I know. Sorry. Hey, I know what you need. Follow me!"

Pepe led Cesar across the street to the general store. "You need a beer, but not a 40-ouncer, okay?" Pepe asked rhetorically. "Just a 12oz can. Don't

124

drink all of it either—" he said, following him to the refrigerator—"just half. It'll help with your symptoms until you get medication again from the doctor."

They walked to the cash register. Cesar waited in line. Pepe went over to the side, pulling a comic from a stand and began flipping its pages.

"What are you doing?" Cesar asked, noticing Pepe scanning the comic book.

"Looking at the pictures."

"You're not going to read it?"

"No," he said, "I don't know how to read, so I just look at the funny drawings."

Because Cesar was broke, Pepe had to buy the beer. They walked back to *Nueva Vida*.

"How come you can't read?" Cesar asked.

"The specialist said I have a learning disability. And something called 'dyslexia.'"

Frustrated with his son's performance, and tired of listening to his son complain, Pepe's father allowed him to stop attending school in 3rd grade. "You can be of use to me at the center," he said to Pepe. "You won't need reading there."

A few days later it occurred to Cesar that he could teach Pepe to read.

Perhaps Cesar felt obliged to help because Pepe had helped him? Perhaps Cesar was a nice guy with a soft heart for children?

"Come outside with me, *chingado*," he told Pepe, taking some of Roberto's old newspapers from a pile. They sat side-by-side on the patio. Pepe sat quietly. "What's this letter here?" he said, pointing at a capitalized "A" in the newspaper.

"Uh, I don't know."

"Okay," Cesar said, "don't worry. We'll start from the beginning."

Cesar could focus on Pepe, unlike schoolteachers who were restricted by the need to help other students. Day after day he had Pepe work with him, despite Pepe's stalling. "I think Carmen's calling me," Pepe said once during a session. "I don't hear anything," Cesar said. "Can I go to the bathroom?" Pepe asked Cesar all the time.

Cesar had him circle every "a" he could find in a paragraph, then the "e's," until Pepe could identify all of the vowels and sound them out. Once Pepe mastered the vowels, Cesar repeated his instructional technique with the consonants.

Carmen was pleasantly surprised by Cesar's commitment and passion. As a counselor, she understood the effects of positive reinforcement. "You're doing an excellent job with Pepe," she said to him one day. "Oh and 'Scarface' doesn't suit you anymore. From now on I'm calling you, *el Profe* (the Professor)."

Cesar's pedagogy was unconventional, but it worked. While teaching Pepe, Cesar learned many things about himself. With a purpose, he could be patient, and stay still for once. He was capable of trusting another person. Indirectly, Pepe helped Cesar kick his drug habit. Cesar didn't have time to obsess about drugs, with his mind constantly thinking of what literature to use, or what words to introduce as new vocabulary. Cesar overheard Puppet and the other *malandros* at *Nueva Vida* call him, "soft." Whatever, he thought. I know I'm not "soft."

During hot summer days, residents of Ciudad Juarez take refuge from the heat in their homes. After *la comida*, or late lunch, they take a power *siesta*. A *siesta* renews everyone's alertness and strength to finish the day. Trying to do anything else is hellish. Ciudad Juarez was scorching. The temperature was 113 degrees Fahrenheit.

Walking out of *Nueva Vida,* Cesar felt like he'd been pressed by a hot iron. He'd run out of cigarettes, and midday was as good as any other time to go across the street. As much as he tried, he couldn't fall asleep during the day.

Cesar crossed the street. The neighborhood looked deserted. Cesar stepped inside the general store. The owner was sitting behind the cash register. A wood panel about three inches thick carved with names and tag monikers, served as his countertop. He looks miserable, Cesar thought, getting a closer look at the man. The man's face was pale and clammy, with sweat falling below his sideburns. A little oscillating fan set on high hung on a wall to the owner's left.

"Can I help you?" he said, staring at Cesar with a look of repulsion.

"Some Fiesta cigarettes," he said. Fuck-you too, old man, Cesar thought.

The man turned around. He reached for a carton of Fiesta cigarettes that was inside a top cabinet. He struggled, trying to pull out a single pack. To pass the time, Cesar looked at magazine covers displayed on a stand to his left. He saw Pepe's comic book, the one he saw Pepe select from the stand as an illiterate boy. Over two months had passed since that day, and since the day of his overdose. Through it all, Cesar had stayed sober.

The storeowner placed the pack on the countertop.

"That'll be seventy-five pesos," he said.

"Oh and this comic book also." Cesar and Pepe had made substantial progress. Pepe was now reading short sentences. This will be perfect, Cesar thought, holding the comic in front of him with both hands. Pepe will finally get to see what he's been missing.

Cesar headed for the store exit. He pushed the door open, getting blinded by the sun. He put his head down to avoid having to squint. He held the comic book in front of him again, flipping the cover and beginning to read. He walked onto the sidewalk. The street was silent. Cesar's chuckles echoed along the boulevard. A few steps from the center, halfway across the street, Cesar was startled by loud noises: Clunk! Clunk!

Cesar took his eyes off the comic book, recognizing the sound of car doors being slammed. Staring at Cesar from outside their sport utility vehicles was a group of masked men, with *cuernos de chivo* (AK-47's) hanging from their shoulders. Cesar's heart jumped, beating faster than it ever had.

"That's one of them!" the leader said. "¡*Mátenlo!*"

One of the masked men grabbed a .45 caliber Glock from his belt line. Cesar's pupils dilated and blood rushed to his legs. He was in full flight before the assassin could level his pistol. He sprinted past the general store, clutching Pepe's comic book like a track and field baton. The shop was a death trap. It had no back door. The end of the street block was Cesar's best option. Running for his life, Cesar desperately hoped he could corner the block and be out of sight before the killer took his shot. Bang!

Over an hour later:

"What do we have here, Ortiz?" Martinez, the lead Investigator, asked a portly Officer standing in front of *Nueva Vida.*

"Multiple homicide scene, sir," he said. "The proprietor is inside with his son."

"How many?"

"Well, sir—" he said, wiping his sweaty brow with a white handkerchief. The temperature had dropped to 100 degrees—"there's twelve inside the house, including the owner's son. They were all killed execution style. The owner has identified one of them, a female, as his counselor, and the ten others were patients he said. Oh and there's one over there." Ortiz pointed behind Martinez to a corpse that laid face down near the street corner.

Martinez walked slowly toward Cesar's body. He stared at the corpse, examining entry wounds with scientific eyes. "One shot to the back," he said. He crouched. With a couple of fingers, he positioned the back of Cesar's head directly below his gaze. "And there's the love tap," he said, seeing a gaping hole in the skull. He scanned around the body for evidence. A few feet away, he noticed something on the floor. He stood, walked toward the object, and picked it up. It was Pepe's comic.

Ortiz heard Martinez chuckling, walking back to the scene of the crime.

"What do you have there, sir?" Ortiz asked.

"It's a comic book."

"Want to go inside now, sir?"

"Why?" Martinez asked, laughing, with his eyes on the page. "We got a recovering *Telenovela* star in there or something?"

"Nah," Ortiz said, "just a bunch of filthy *malandros*."

The Punishment

Jose Fernandez couldn't believe how fast it all happened. He was living in San Jose, California with Jesus, a friend from his hometown, Meoqui. He was working odd jobs, sending very little money to Valentina, his wife, who was back in Mexico with their two children, Veronica and Jose Jr. It seemed like only a brief moment passed. To his dismay, his family was with him again, stuffing Jesus' living room with three additional people.

"Why in the hell did you leave Meoqui, Valentina?" Jose asked as they sat in Jesus' backyard. "You should've called me. Don't you know how dangerous it was?"

The sun had set, leaving behind a hot Bay Area day in July for the onshore breeze to cool.

"It was more dangerous to stay. There's no future for us in Mexico."

"Okay, but why didn't you wait? Why did you have to come so,"—he paced nervously craving a drink—"so, unexpectedly?"

"Unexpectedly?" Valentina asked rhetorically. "Two years I've heard you say you'd save enough money to pay our way to *el Norte*. And have you?" Her head tilted slightly back to the right. She raised her left eyebrow in anticipation of his response.

"Damn it, Valentina! I spent the money I've made on food, rent, and—"

"And beer," Valentina said, cutting Jose off.

With incredulity, he listened to Valentina tell him how five nights before her childhood friend, Carmen, came over to the house. Carmen had asked Valentina to join her own family, husband Chuy and their three kids, on an illegal crossing into El Paso. In

El Paso they'd all try to evade Immigration once again at the airport, taking a flight to Los Angeles.

Valentina, deciding it was now or never, had packed a bag of clothes, telling Jr. and Veronica to keep their northbound trip a secret.

"Why a secret?" Jose asked her.

"You think I wanted your mom and dad, your sisters, discouraging me?"

You didn't want them discouraging you, but I sure did, Jose thought.

"Chuy and Carmen were only in Meoqui for a few days on account of Chuy's sick mother," she said. "They assured me they'd crossed the border numerous times and knew how to avoid *la migra* without a Coyote."

Apart from Valentina's newly discovered audacity, which Jose had to squash as soon as possible, money was his other concern. "But where did you get the money to pay for the bus and train ride to Juarez?" he asked. "The flight from El Paso to Los Angeles?"

"From Chuy of course," she said calmly with an undertone of confidence. "He made plenty of money working in Los Angeles. He told me not to worry, to pay him back when we can..."

Damn him, Jose thought. How dare he meddle? Forcing me to drive to Los Angeles. He must think he's some sort of saint, getting Valentina and the kids safely to Los Angeles. Least he could've done is dropped them off. And now I owe him money!

"...which I know we can do," Valentina continued. She stopped talking noticing Jose wasn't looking at her. "Jose," she said, "you listening?"

"Oh," he said, "yeah. Easy for you to say. Money in California is hard to come by!"

Jose listened unresponsively to the rest of Valentina's version of what happened en route. How she and the kids crossed the Rio Grande in the middle of the day, holding onto each other and the inner tube pulled by Chuy. How they sweated profusely because of the desert heat, wondering if *la migra* would catch them, incarcerate and deport them back to Mexico. Having crossed the border unscathed many times, it all sounded trivial to Jose, despite Valentina's efforts to make it harrowing.

Jose spent the rest of the week pissed off. Valentina had ruined his carefree existence, working part time, just enough to pay rent to his friend, eat, and fund his drinking. At twenty-nine he still had at least a decade's worth of partying before a lifetime of servitude to his wife. He was used to his freedom. Ten years of marriage to Valentina hadn't taken away his ability come and go as he pleased. It wouldn't start now, even if the marriage had arrived in America like a cheap Made in Mexico package.

The Fernandez's first place of their own, an apartment on Sunny Lane, was a one bedroom. It had a kitchen with a small nook to fit a table for four, and the living room was carpeted. The bathroom had a shower *and* a tub. The amenities within the complex included a grimy pool and a moldy laundry room. It was vastly superior to the one bedroom home they left behind in Chihuahua.

Jose figured the apartment on Sunny Lane would do. The rent of $600 dollars a month was more than he could afford with his single paycheck, even with the extra hours he'd procured with the help of Jesus, who was a good friend of the shift supervisor. Jose didn't want to work full time, especially the night shift. It was the only way he could prove to Valentina that after the rent expense, there wasn't enough left over for groceries, and especially not enough for her to stay home with the kids. I'll be damned if I'm the only one who works around here, he thought.

"What about the kids?" Valentina asked. "Who'll watch them?"

"Veronica is almost eleven," Jose said. "She's old enough to look after Jr."

"Can't you get a second job?" she asked, appealing desperately to Jose's better judgment. "They'd have to be alone at night. Trapped inside like prisoners. What if someone comes knocking at the door? What if the authorities investigate? They've just started learning English in school!"

"You didn't think about all this, did you? *Pero muy brava te dejaste venir a los Estados Unidos* (But you were brave in coming to the United States). Now you see—"

"*Pero Jose—*"

"*¡Pero nada, Valentina!* Enough already."

He stared her down, reminding her who owned the *cojones*.

"The matter is settled," Jose said. "The two of us will work. Jesus went out of his way to convince the supervisor to add you to the cleaning crew. We're saving money on gas by working together and we can use your check to pay for the rest of our bills. Maybe we'll even have enough left over for a family outing once in awhile."

Three years later, downtrodden and tired, Jose got in his '75 Buick Riviera on a Saturday morning in February. The temperature inside the vehicle was only a few degrees warmer than outside. Before inserting his key into the ignition, Jose made a loose fist and blew warm air in the chamber made by his fingers. It only took him three turns of the key and four pumps of the gas pedal to start the car. "You cut me a break today you piece of shit," Jose said outloud.

Jose had several friends in San Jose that he enjoyed killing time with. But Jesus was still his main man. Arriving at Jesus' house, he felt once again free of his chain, Valentina and the kids. A chain that was tightening with each additional day the family spent in America. Jesus' wife, Yesenia, answered his knocks.

"Oh," she said, "it's you, Jose. *Pasa.*"

She moved to the side so he could enter.

"*¿Y Jesus?*" he asked.

"He's getting ready. How's Valentina?"

"She's fine. With the kids."

"You should bring her next time. The two of us can chat while you and Jesus hang out."

Not a chance, Jose thought. "She doesn't like to impose. The kids can be a handful."

"She won't be imposing. Veronica and Jr. can watch television in the living room. Make all the noise they want."

Jesus came out of the bedroom, stuffing the bottom of his long-sleeve flannel shirt into his pants.

"You pestering Jose again, Yesenia?" he asked authoritatively. Jesus walked right past her.

"I was just saying to him—"

"How are you, *compadre*?" Jesus asked, interrupting his wife.

"Good," Jose said, "and you?"

"Good, good," he said. "Come, let's go outside."

Jesus opened the door to the backyard with a case of beer in hand, offering one to Jose, leaving Yesenia behind like an ephemeral apparition.

"Put on a jacket, Jesus!" she said. "It's cold outside!"

"Can you bring it to me?" Jesus asked rhetorically.

They sat on a pair of folded-out metal chairs with their arms crossed. It was a little after eleven in the morning. Jose cracked open his Budweiser, unable to resist the temptation any longer.

"How's work?" Jose asked after taking a hard swig.

"Same shit," Jesus said. "I may finally get placed on the day crew."

"That's great news."

"Yeah, we'll see. Never worked so hard before in my life."

Jesus unclasped his arms, reached down, and grabbed his beer. Just then Yesenia appeared, holding Jesus' jacket an arm's length outside the backyard door, keeping the rest of her body warm inside the house.

"Bring it to me," Jesus said, looking up at her, smirking.

"No!" she said playfully. "It's cold out there."

"But *mi amor*, if I get up my seat will get cold. You don't want my *nalgas* to freeze again, do you?"

Jose chuckled. Jesus did his best not to laugh, holding a straight face.

"*¡Ay, Jesus!*" she said, dashing out the door, delivering the jacket, and running back inside.

"That's my girl!" Jesus said approvingly. "See, that's why I love you so much. Always taking care of me."

Yesenia closed the door, saying nothing in response.

Jose took another swig. "Valentina asked me to teach her to drive. I almost spit out my beer.

What's with our women in this country? They want to be like the *gabachas*, driving all over the place, getting their hair and nails done every week, eating *ese Mac Donal* they see on T.V. She says the kids enjoy going there, eating those fucking hamburgers—"

"Which ones, *compadre*?" Jesus asked, opening his can of beer. He took three swigs.

"You know," Jose said, "those ones they call, 'Big Macs.' I know what she's doing. That Valentina thinks she's smart, but she's not fooling me."

"What do you mean, *compa*?"

"She's trying to stop cooking!" Jose said demonstratively. He was so upset he chugged down the rest of his beer. With his jacket sleeve, he wiped the liquid left on his lips.

"*¿Otra cerveza, compa?*"

By 1:00 p.m. the pair had drunk six beers each and had talked all kinds of mess about immigrant life. They cursed out their *gringo* employers, calling them slave masters. They damned to hell the negative influences of American culture on Mexican children and ridiculed *gringo* men for failing to keep *gringa* women in check.

"They say the *gabacho* has a small penis," Jose said, smiling wide.

"Who says, *compa*?"

"Some *jotos* at work."

They laughed so hysterically that Jesus peed a dribble in his pants.

"Come," Jesus said. "Let's go buy some more *cerveza.*"

"I'll drive," Jose said.

The two men walked back inside. Yesenia was in the kitchen cooking a meal. She moved her wooden spoon with some effort across a pan full of ground beef and chopped potato. Without noticing her, Jesus and Jose walked by, heading for the living room.

"Jesus," Yesenia said, "where are you going?"

Jesus stood still annoyed at his wife for detaining them. "To get some more beer with Jose."

"Lunch is almost ready. I made *carne molida con papa burritos.* You and Jose should eat before you go out."

"We're not hungry," Jesus said dismissively.

"But Jesus," she said, "you've been drinking on an empty stomach. You shouldn't drive like that."

"I'm not!" he said. "Jose's driving, okay? And besides I didn't ask for your permission."

Clutching his belt, Jesus waited for any backtalk from his woman. *"Vamonos compadre,"* he said a moment later to Jose, hearing only the sounds of movement in the kitchen.

Driving along Story Road in San Jose's east side, Jose's Buick added to the mix of foul smells. Vietnamese grocery stores and noodle shops, one at every street corner, sickened Jose. "That's another thing," he said seemingly perturbed, restarting the conversation they left back at the house.

"What's that?" Jesus asked.

"In Chihuahua, we don't have to smell this nasty food the *Chinos* cook in their restaurants."

Jesus laughed. *"Ay, compadre,"* he said. "They're not actually *Chino.* They're *Vietnamita.* And they make tasty *caldos.* You don't get out much, do you?"

"Bah!" Jose said, belching. "I miss Mexico, is all I'm saying. I've been here three years and I don't see what's so great about this country. Valentina and I've made zero progress. All we do is work to pay bills. Take this little drive we're having right now.

Sure we've had a few drinks. You think anybody would care back in Mexico? Here, *la chota* sees you swerve a little and they think you can't handle a car. Pull you over for no fucking reason. Just because you're Mexican."

Just then a San Jose Police cruiser pulled up behind Jose. The flash and wail of its siren alarmed the men.

"*¡A la madre!*" (Oh, mother fucker!) Jesus said. "You really did it this time, *compadre*. You've managed to conjure up *la chota* (the cops) out of thin air. We're fucked!"

Though he was initially stopped for a malfunctioning taillight, Jose spent the rest of the weekend in jail. On Monday he pled guilty before a judge for driving under the influence, twice the legal limit, and his license was suspended, a license he'd obtained using a fake green card. Luckily he was released a couple of hours before work. Jesus, accompanied by Valentina, picked him up from the courthouse and drove him to the impound lot. They parked just outside the gate and got out.

"I owe you big time," Jose said to Jesus, taking from him three hundred dollars, the cost to get his car out. "I'll pay you back as soon as I can."

"It's the least I can do," Jesus said. "It was my fault, suggesting we buy more beer after sharing a twelve pack."

"Nah," Jose said. "If you hadn't, I would've done it myself."

Valentina was livid. Her serious and reddened countenance made Jesus uncomfortable.

"I'll see you later, *compadre*," he said, walking away quickly.

As soon as Jesus was out of range, Valentina went on the offensive.

"You happy now?" she asked Jose with contempt.

"Don't start, Valentina," Jose said impatiently, walking toward the pay booth.

It took fifteen minutes for the car to be driven out. The entire time Jose kept his distance from Valentina. Despite a suspended license, he took his place behind the steering wheel. Once in the vehicle with his wife, Jose felt like an injured animal, cornered by a smaller, yet healthier enemy. The couple had a little over an hour before work. Jose wanted to forget the weekend, get home and shower, and get the jail funk off his skin. Valentina tossed the shit back in his face.

"Did they ask you for papers?" she asked.

"No," he said, lying. The police interpreter had in fact asked him for documentation to prove his legal status in the country. He'd told the man he'd left his green card at home, presenting only his driver's license.

"They fingerprint you?"

"Yes."

"They photograph you?"

"Yes, Valentina! You going to keep asking me questions like the goddamn police, or what? Isn't what I've been through enough?"

"What *you've* been through? What about me? What about what your children have been through?"

She had more on her mind than this one incident. Jose's drinking was out of control. Over the past several months his temper had often flared beyond its usual output. He'd scolded Veronica for wearing make-up and had whipped Jr. with a belt for getting in trouble at school. He'd punched a hole in the wall arguing with Valentina.

"And whose fault is that?" Jose asked. "If you'd stayed in Mexico with the kids like I wanted, none of this would've happened. I'd be back there with you right now, enjoying my life!"

They reached their apartment on Sunny Lane. Jose parked haphazardly and poorly. The two stormed inside. Jose slammed the door, shaking the entire place.

"So this is what it's been about?" Valentina asked. The entire time we've been here you've resented what I did for our kids? The risk I took to give them a better life, something you couldn't provide for them!"

Instead of running toward their father, happy to have him back, Veronica and Jr. sat frozen on the couch. The verbal bullets were flying. Their parents argued for another twenty minutes. Even as their father showered, their mother shouted at him from outside the curtain. Jr. turned up the television to drown out the noise. Wearing their work clothes, Jose and Valentina walked into the living room. Their dad ploughed across the room, stopping at the door to make one final show of his power.

"We're not living here for the rest of our lives!" Jose said with his index finger pointing to the ground. "We're going back to Chihuahua, and soon! Hurry up, Valentina." He stepped out, slamming the door, leaving Valentina, Veronica, and Jr., speechless.

Two Months Later:

Two white men in suits, executives from the human resources department, rounded up all of the undocumented Mexicans in the lobby of the corporate offices and fired them all. Jesus stared at his *compadre* Jose in disbelief. Jose was elated. This was the opportunity he'd been waiting for. The door to his escape from the U.S. had opened. He feigned concern around the others, and especially around Valentina. Jesus' friend, the night supervisor, and his accomplice, a manager unbeknownst to the cleaning crew, had been taken into custody. They'd hired illegals, paying them less than the minimum wage, pocketing the difference.

Jose's words two months earlier, said in the heat of the battle with his wife after his incarceration, had proved to be prophetic. With both of them out of a job and with no savings, the bills would soon mount. If he stalled long enough, Jose would finally get his wish and be back in his hometown, roaming free again from *cantina* to *cantina,* fishing without stupid licenses or permits, and hanging out on street corners with his friends without being harassed by police.

The eviction letter came a week after the first of the month. Jose read it first then handed it to Valentina. She held the letter as if it were a death sentence for her and her children.

"We'll find somewhere to live," she said desperately.

"Yeah," Jose said, "where?"

"With Jesus maybe."

"He's in the same situation. Broke. You think he wants another family in his home right now? No, Valentina. I don't see any other way." He was calm, speaking carefully so as not to spark suspicion.

"What about those shelters *el Padre Tomas* talks about in his after mass announcements?" she asked, biting her nails. "We could stay in one of those until we find employment."

"Valentina," he said convincingly, "both Jesus and I have been actively looking for employment.

We're not good with our hands, so we can't do construction. Standing on a corner, waiting like dogs for a *gabacho* to invite us onto his truck won't cut it. Even if I were chosen, gardening doesn't pay enough to support a family of four. Everywhere else they ask for papers. They don't allow you to stay in a shelter forever, do they?"

Jesus had indeed gone out to look for work each day. But Jose hadn't. He left early in the morning, and drove to the library where he'd read Spanish literature, or to the park, where he'd play games of handball until he got tired. He even left Valentina's packed lunch intact a few times, claiming he'd been too busy to eat.

Taking advantage of her pensive look, Jose added an additional comment to crush her spirit.

"You know, Valentina," he said, "we were very lucky that day. Those executives could've called *la migra.* Instead of sitting here right now, you and I could be in a holding tank, waiting to be flown to the border. Where would that have left Veronica and Jr.?"

Valentina looked worried. His words had found their mark.

"It's just not fair, Jose," she said. "The kids are doing well in school. They're learning English so fast. And they like it here. I heard in the news that President Reagan may soon reform the Immigration laws. Can you imagine? Our children would have a chance at the American dream."

"Ay, Valentina," he said softly, shaking his head. "It's political rhetoric. The man is trying to score points with liberal voters. When have politicians ever kept their promises?"

The Fernandez's sold all of their furniture two weeks later, keeping only their clothes, photo albums, and other sentimental trinkets. What they could fit in the Buick. A mechanic friend of Jose tuned up his car for free. It was spring, and they would have good weather to drive through southern Californian and Mexican deserts.

On a perfect Saturday in April, outside of the apartment on Sunny Lane, the Fernandez's friends gathered to say goodbye. There was *Raymundo,* the twenty-year-old Mexican-American *cholo* from number eighteen upstairs and *Tino* and *Berta*, the Nicaraguan couple from number six across the hall from the Fernandez's now empty place, number eight. Yesenia was there without Jesus. He had to work.

Jesus had just started his new job at a Mexican *Mercado.* "Jesus has more resources!" Jose said to Valentina. As a last ditch effort, Valentina had asked Yesenia to ask Jesus if he could talk to the manager at the *Mercado*, and see if he could hire one more. "Do me a favor, *compadre*," he said to Jesus. "Tell your wife they're not hiring." And just like that, Jose's punishment in America was finished.

Near the edge of the sidewalk, Valentina hugged everyone. Her eyes were beginning to water. With a gloating smile, Jose shook hands, hugging Yesenia, telling her to say goodbye to Jesus for him. Jr. and Veronica got in the car, looking at their American neighborhood one last time.

The family waved goodbye and drove off.

"Kids, we go back to a place where we belong. Mexico. *¡Nuestra patria!*"

"You never gave it a chance," Valentina said sobbing, as Veronica and Jr. cried in the back.

El Consentido

Sammy didn't even get up as his older brother, Fernando, walked through the door. His parents *were* standing, welcoming Fernando back home. Sitting on the couch, he tried to keep looking at the television, but curiosity compelled Sammy to see how happy his parents were. Lourdes, their mother, was glowing like the Our Lady of Guadalupe candle she had lit before the framed image of Fernando that rested on the entertainment center. In the picture, Fernando's distinct Mexican features, brown face, high cheekbones, thin moustache, slightly slanted black eyes, expressed pride under the formal U.S. Marine Corps dress hat. Carlos, their father, normally stoic around his children, smirked while holding his arms out for an embrace. To Sammy, his parents' reaction confirmed that nothing had change. Fernando was still *el consentido*, or their favorite.

"Don't get up on account of me, lazy," Fernando said, giving Sammy a dirty look.

"Okay," Sammy said smartly, "I won't."

"Mira este mal educado," or "Check out this poorly educated," Fernando said to his mother, shaking his head. He looked briefly at his father. "If I was this ill-mannered at his age you would've pulled out your belt."

Carlos shrugged.

"Let him be, *mijo*," Lourdes said to Fernando. *"Andale*, go drop off your gear and come to the kitchen. I made your favorite, *caldo de pollo*."

After hugging his father, Fernando kissed his mother's cheek. He got in front of Sammy, blocking his view. Fernando stood there daring Sammy to stand. Sammy stood quickly, frustrated at having to look around Fernando's scrawny legs. Without speaking, the two brothers challenged each other for space, facing only millimeters apart. Tension filled the room. With a look of concern, Lourdes took a step forward. Carlos tapped her shoulder gently. "Wait," he said. Suddenly Sammy and Fernando burst into laughter, ending the standoff.

"Let me help you with that, big brother," Sammy said, taking a duffel bag from Fernando.

"Thanks, little brother," Fernando said. "You were more convincing this time. You didn't even blink." The two walked out of the living room heading to their shared bedroom.

"This bag is heavy!" Sammy said. "You pack a tank in here, or what?" They left their parents alone, Carlos smiling, and Lourdes weeping joyfully.

The kitchen was warm and damp. Lourdes had prepared dinner an hour before. Condensation had formed on the windows from the boiling vegetable and chicken stock. The plastic placemats on the table were sweaty. Lourdes hustled into the kitchen, turning the stove on low to reheat the *caldo*. From a cabinet she reached for a *comal* and set it on top of a flaming burner. She placed four cold tortillas on the *comal* and waited, passing the time thinking of *Puerto Nuevo*. She missed her hometown in Baja. Carlos had refused driving her there, and prohibited Lourdes from visiting alone because of Tijuana's drug violence.

"Smells good in here, *ama*," Ferndando said, snapping Lourdes out of her reverie.

"*Gracias, mijo,*" she said. "Where's your brother?"

"He'll be here in a minute. He's checking himself out in the mirror again. Mr. *Guapo* has to look good even for dinner."

"And your dad?"

"On the computer messing with his Mp3 collection. He's really into his music."

"No, not his music," Lourdes said. "More like keeping to himself. As if he needed help with that."

"Sorry," Fernando said. His mother had always been candid with him. The seven months he'd spent in Iraq had been rough. He wasn't ready to be back, listening to his mother complain about his father. He felt he should say something more: "He'll get bored and move onto something else—"

"Who'll get bored and move onto something else?" Carlos asked, stepping into the kitchen and sitting at the head of the table.

"We were just talking about Sammy," Fernando said lying, avoiding eye contact with his father. "He'll get tired of sitting around and go find a job. Maybe move out someday."

"Oh, I see," Carlos said now seemingly uninterested. *"Andale, Vieja,"* he said to Lourdes, nodding toward the stove. "Serve your son some *caldo*."

Conditioned to oblige, Lourdes sprang out of her chair like a circus animal. "How many tortillas do you want, Fernando?" she asked.

After dinner Sammy unbuttoned his pants to let his gut expand comfortably. Fernando and Carlos loosened their belts. Lourdes was just starting to eat. Sammy felt like antagonizing Fernando.

"So how's the Iraq occupation coming along?" he asked with a straight face.

It was late in the war, when all of America, except Washington, had acknowledged that there were no weapons of mass destruction. Fernando had done one previous tour. He'd missed the invasion, joining the marines out of high school in 2004.

"Don't start, Sammy. Talk to me when *you* find a purpose in life." As Fernando talked, Lourdes placed a meatless chicken bone on her placemat. Fernando paused, grabbing a couple of napkins from where they were laid neatly stacked. He handed them to his mother, earning a look of gratitude from her. "No career is perfect, you know!" Fernando said.

"I'll never make killing for The Man my purpose in life," Sammy said assertively, wishing he'd thought to be considerate.

Fernando ignored him. Sammy was perturbed that he couldn't bait Fernando into an argument.

"I picked up rank in Iraq," Fernando said humbly. "I'm a Sergeant now. And I met the qualifications to be a brown belt instructor."

Fucking show off, Sammy thought. Stop being such a tool.

"Mijo el Sargento," Carlos said shifting forward in his chair, reaching for the toothpick dispenser and winking at Fernando.

"That's wonderful news, *mijo*," Lourdes said. "Your dreams are coming true." She set her spoon gently in the almost empty bowl, signaling her capitulation. She'd eaten fast.

Attentive to his mother, Fernando grabbed the toothpick dispenser, taking a toothpick out and handing it to his mother across the table.

Nice going, Sammy thought sarcastically, staring at his brother with fury in his eyes. Next you'll be taking her plate to the sink.

"If I re-enlist," Fernando said, pausing to catch a glimpse of his mother's expression, "I know I can make Staff Sergeant."

"¿Uuuy, pues cuantos Sargentos hay?" or "Dang, well how many Sergeants are there?" Lourdes asked jovially, saving Fernando from presenting a rehearsed argument in favor of continuing his military career.

Initially Lourdes had opposed Fernando's enlistment, telling him to be patient. "You'll get your green card in due time," she'd said. "You don't need the military's help becoming a legal resident." Like any mother she was fearful. The images of marines coming home in body bags lingered in her mind.

"¿Y si te matan?" or "What if they kill you?" she said, as the family watched television a year into Operation Iraqi Freedom. "What would I do without you?"

"You have Sammy, Mom," Fernando said, making a consolation prize out of his brother.

"Let him go, Lourdes," Carlos said. "It'll make a man out of him."

Fernando would've gone without his mother's approval. The recruiter had made sense. For a Mexican with a temporary green card, joining the military was a logical decision. The benefits: job training, upward mobility, a chance at a pension, assistance with becoming a legal resident, far outweighed the risks. Sammy was on his side for once. He'd supported Fernando's choice.

"Actually, *ama*," Fernando said, "there are several more Sergeant ranks. There's Staff Sergeant, Gunnery Sergeant, Master—"

"Alright already!" Sammy said. "We get the point."

The Santa Ana winds were vicious the night Sammy and Fernando set out, howling louder than the coyotes of the San Luis Rey River. It was warm for November, but the conditions were typical for Southern California. Holding onto his cowboy hat, Fernando stepped out of the two-bedroom duplex his parents rented in Oceanside. Sammy was right behind with his hands in his pockets.

"Te ves como un pendejo," or "You look like a dumbass," Fernando said to him. "How can you go to a Rodeo wearing baggy jeans and sneakers?"

"¿Y tu, güey? (And you, jackass?) Sammy asked. "You look like a *pinche paisa* (fucking countryman) with those boots and tight pants."

"Yeah," Fernando said, "except I'll be dressed like everyone else."

They had borrowed their father's truck for the night out, a brand new 2010 Ford Tundra. Despite the cross gusting winds, the vehicle rode steady with Fernando at the wheel. Sammy let down his window and turned up the stereo, blasting sounds of *Narco corridos* into their quiet neighborhood.

"You deaf?" Fernando asked, turning the volume down immediately.

"What the hell?" Sammy asked.

Fernando delayed a response. A week had passed since his arrival, enough time in his mind to resume his main brotherly role, that of mentor. He wanted to start slow, avoid smothering Sammy, and make sure he wasn't shell-shocked. In his estimation, the Warrior Transition briefs at Pendleton had been useless. "Don't hit your spouse...don't blow all your money on a new motorcycle...if you're stressed go see...," the instructor had said.

"Listen, Sammy," Fernando said, taking a quick look at him, "I think it's time you look for a job. Help *ama y apa* with some of the bills."

"You gonna get all Mr. Responsible with me too?" Sammy asked. "Isn't putting on a show for mom and dad, enough?"

"What are you talking about? Show? What show?"

"Getting all high and mighty, Mr. War Hero. So you kicked in a few doors. Shot at"—he made quotation marks with his fingers—"insurgents. So what? Now you're back here in So. Cal. A Beaner, just like the rest of us."

Fernando eased off the gas pedal to focus on talking. The conversation was not headed in the direction he'd hoped for. Instead of giving Sammy advice on the job market, information he'd received only days before on base, he had to change the topic.

"Why the huge chip on your shoulder, Sammy? You had everything you needed. Mom and dad fed you everyday. Sent you to school with nice clothes. Better than what I had. And you were born here! You could be in college right now, as smart as you are."

"Yeah," he said, chuckling, "I've not bought in just yet."

"That's the problem with you. You think everything is a joke."

Not everything, Sammy thought. Just you.

"You squander your time, hanging out with those *pendejos* from the block, drinking in the middle of the day. You should be working. Or at least going to Junior College!"

"I'll think about it," Sammy said. "Can we stop all this serious shit? We're almost there."

The Show Palace parking lot smelled like cheap perfume and cologne. The boot heels of people walking to the entrance made thudding sounds, striking the cement ground. It was dark. The strip mall was poorly lit. Sammy and Fernando got out of their vehicle and were immediately greeted by a stray Mexican *grito: ¡Aaaay-yaaa-yay!*

"*Oye,*" or "Listen," Fernando said to Sammy, scanning several rows of parked cars. "Some *loco* out there is already drunk."

"Or high," Sammy said, combing his hair back one last time. He threw his comb inside the truck and slammed the door. "Let's go."

Fernando walked inside the club first, tucking a wristband he'd received at the door under his cuff, identifying him as above the legal age to purchase alcohol. Sammy was twenty, five years younger than his brother, and he resented being inside untagged. Without a wristband, he'd suffer discriminating stares from older women. Eighteen and nineteen-year-olds no longer interested him. Without a cold beer in hand, he'd also feel awkward around women.

The place was bumping. The wooden dance floor bounced. Some couples danced tightly, sliding side to side. Others were doing *quebradita*; men swung and slung their ladies dangerously across the dance floor. Fernando went straight for the bar, leaving Sammy in the company of several Mexicans dressed as cowboys, doing their best to appear *valiente.* Sammy looked to his right and was met by the ugly face of a fair-complexioned *Norteño,* a northern Mexican, giving him a mean look. What are you fucking looking at? Sammy thought. Disgusted, he turned his head away slowly, back toward the dance floor.

Sammy's night endured like a drought. He was sober and isolated most of the time. Women were intrigued by his looks. He had the face of a pretty boy, soft and effeminate, stood five-foot-eleven, and had an athletic body. But he couldn't compete for women with most of the men there. He was shy when not buzzed, possessed two left dancing feet, and was dressed too casually. He tried speaking to a beautiful and slender lady near the bar. He tried flirting with her. She was led away smiling by the confident hand of a *paisa,* and lost in the vortex of the dance floor. Before he gave up, he tried a couple more times with the same outcome.

Meanwhile Fernando came and went. He checked in with Sammy occasionally, introducing his dance partners like trophies he'd just won. Fuck this! Sammy thought, seeing Fernando having a great time. Let's make things a little more interesting.

To challenge Fernando, Sammy picked the biggest Mexican he could find at the Show Palace. He walked around and through crowds with purpose until he found his mark. Towering like a saguaro cactus with arms thick as barrels, the man never saw Sammy coming.

The *paisa* screamed at Sammy after the bump: "Watch where you're going, *pendejo!*"

Sammy had spilled beer all over the *paisa's* hand. Sammy turned around. Two other males and a female, most likely the *paisa's* friends, Sammy assumed, stared at him.

"Who you calling *pendejo, cabron?*" Sammy asked. He looked briefly around the club, trying to spot Fernando. He saw Fernando talking to a couple of women nearby. Relieved, he stood taller and clenched his fists.

"I'm calling you a *pendejo, güey,*" he said, shoving Sammy.

"Pinche joto culero," or "Fucking gay asshole," Sammy said, shoving him back.

Sammy knew those three words stringed together would do the job. Within seconds, they were engaged in combat. Sammy connected a few times, swinging like a welterweight, electing volume over force. But it wasn't enough. He caught a wicked right hand on the cheek that dropped him to the ground. Sammy covered up, feeling boot tips hammering into his midsection.

Fernando noticed the commotion. When he saw Sammy on the floor, his heart began beating rapidly. The sound of an AK-47 burst from a *Narco-corrido* song propelled Fernando into action. He was back in Iraq and Sammy was a wounded brother. As he moved through the crowd swiftly and adeptly, *sombreros* morphed into headscarves. Long sleeve shirts, belts, and jeans transformed into white robes. The bass from the speakers were mortar explosions. The chaos of screaming women injected adrenaline into his bloodstream.

When Fernando regained his senses, he was in handcuffs outside the venue being led into an Oceanside Police Department squad car. "What happened?" Fernando asked the arresting officer on their way to the station.

"Good one," the officer said through the wire mesh.

"No, really. I don't remember."

"You kung-fu-ed the crap out of several men. Hurt one of the bouncers pretty bad."

"What?" Fernando asked incredulously, trying to remember. "Where's my brother? Where's Sammy?"

"On his way home probably. You, my man, are going to jail."

Fernando spent the weekend in jail. He was released Monday afternoon. By then all charges had been dropped, but the damage was done.

The sight of Sammy outside the jailhouse elated Fernando. He was glad Sammy was uninjured with only a small purple bruise on his face. The two embraced. Fernando felt a deep connection to Sammy, as if the intensity from his ordeal channeled through and lit them up like two globe bulbs.

Fernando followed Sammy to the truck. "What the hell happened, Sammy?" he asked. "Why were those people beating on you?"

"The big *paisa* got angry at me for flirting with his girl. Funny thing is she came onto me! She never told me she had a boyfriend."

"Damn, Sammy," Fernando said, smacking the back of his head, "I spent two nights in jail for a *pinche ruca!*"

"But she was a fine ass *ruca!*" He raced to the truck laughing all the way with Fernando giving chase.

While incarcerated, Fernando had plenty of time to think. What would his *ama* and *apa* say about his behavior back at the Show Palace? His running afoul of the law? He'd never done anything so out of character in his life. He also pondered what Sergeant Major Reynolds would do to him. As he was processed, the police informed him someone would contact the Provost Marshal's Office. The Sergeant Major would likely take a chunk out of his ass first thing Tuesday morning.

"Am I in trouble with *ama* and *apa*?" Fernando asked Sammy, looking out his window.

"You kidding me? Sammy asked rhetorically. "You're even more on a pedestal now than you were before!"

"What? How so?"

"That's what brothers are for," he said with a mischievous look. "I told them the truth. I was harassed and assaulted over a simple misunderstanding, and you—" he took his eyes off the road, winking at him; a perfect imitation of their father—"came to my rescue."

"Thanks, *carnal*," Fernando said, grateful.

Fernando had left most of his things in storage. He'd be leaving his parent's house by the end of the month, having found an apartment. When he reported to his battalion the day after his incarceration, the Sergeant Major was waiting.

"You fucked up, Sergeant Sanchez!" the Sergeant Major said.

"Sir," Fernando said, "I was defending my brother."

"Don't give me that 'I was defending my brother' bullshit, Sergeant! You know full-well the ramifications of your conduct."

"But, sir—"

"But nothing, Sergeant! You used deadly force on civilians. You were goddamn lucky you didn't kill anyone. You were jailed, and you failed to report for duty on Monday."

"I'm sorry, sir."

"I'm sorry too, Sergeant. Sorry for what's coming your way."

Two weeks later, Sammy was smoking a joint with neighborhood friends when he saw Fernando pulling up.

"Fuck! Fuck! Fuck!" Fernando said, slamming the door. He pounded on the hood repeatedly.

Sammy jogged across the street. "Whoa, whoa, whoa, big brother," he said, putting his arm around Fernando's shoulders. "You're gonna dent your hood. Why are you so pissed off?"

"Shit happened at work," Fernando said, breathing hard.

"What?"

"Nothing, man. I don't want to talk about it."

"I'm your bro! Who else you gonna tell?"

"Look," Fernando said, "those *cabrones* took away my life, okay! Everything that meant something to me."

"Which *cabrones*?" Sammy asked seemingly very interested. "Let me go fuck 'em up for you."

"The Sergeant Major and his superiors. They stripped me of my rank. I'm back to being a *pinche* Corporal! They also took away my tab. I can't certify anyone anymore to be a brown belt."

Aw, that's too bad, Sammy thought insincerely. "That's fucked up. Why they do that?"

"What do you mean 'why'?" Fernando asked. "*You* were there. You don't remember now? Those *paisas* I handled for you at the Show Palace?"

How could I forget? Sammy thought. That was some of my best work. "Oh, man," Sammy said with a serious face, "I'm really sorry, bro."

"So much for re-enlisting next year," Fernando said with a melancholy stare into empty space. "There's no point to it now with all this crap on my record. I had my future all planned out."

Sammy rejoiced. He wanted to leap into the sky. His brother, *el consentido de sus padres*, had fallen, and the two of them were finally on an equal plane.

"I thought they were my family," Fernando said sighing.

Sammy walked up to Fernando, and put his hand on Fernando's shoulder like a coach talking to a dejected athlete. "See that," Sammy said, pointing at three homies sitting on a porch across the street. "That's your family. *I'm* your family. *Ama* and *Apa* are your family. And *we'll* never let you down!"

The Freight Train

"Hey you tramps get down from there!" my grandpa, Jose, said like an actor practicing a line. "That is what this gringo told me and my friend..."

Grandpa was telling one of his stories again. I'd already heard this one twice, about his days as a migrant worker. Each time, he'd recycle the same gestures, the same facial expressions and tone of voice. For a man nearing his eighty-fourth birthday, he relates images of the past with vivid detail. I often wonder if he's making things up on the fly. No way he remembers what color shirt he was wearing that day. Anyway, this freight train is at the center of this particular flashback. And that was easy enough for me to imagine, lying somewhere on a track like a long stretched-out python.

"*¿Usted sabe de la Depresión?*" he asked.

"Yes, grandpa," I said. "I learned about it in school."

"*Bueno*, in those times the trains would take us everywhere, and we'd get off to work wherever and for whatever because there was nothing."

I sat next to him on the living room sofa, as patiently as is possible for a sixteen-year-old male with A.D.D. The brand new television my father had bought for my *abuelos* was tuned to some *telenovela*. My grandmother was watching it on her love seat. I couldn't help stealing glances occasionally. Mostly to catch sight of the beautiful leading lady they always cast for these shows. Besides, my grandpa is nearly blind from glaucoma. I knew he couldn't see me turn my eyes away.

"Where are you two tramps heading?" grandpa continued. "That is what the gringo asked us after we got down from the platform."

There I was again, sitting on the ground near some train tracks. I was drinking coffee with some white hick in California during the early 1930's. When I first heard grandpa describe this scene it was colorful. I was spending just enough energy now to let it play out in black and white. In my defense, grandpa had worn me out earlier with one of his other stories. What was that one about? I tried remembering. Oh yes, the time he met Pancho Villa as a child.

"We were on our way to Santa Paula *a trabajar el betabel*," he said leaning toward me. His glazed and blood-shot eyes were off by a foot from mine. "Sugar beet."

"Yes, grandpa," I said cuing him.

"We were in Oxnard then," he said very matter of fact, "and we didn't know how far Santa Paula was from there." He raised both his arms with his palms out. His head tilted and his lips scrunched.

My *abuela* was in better shape. Other than her arthritis, she was sharp and mobile for an eighty-year-old. She was knitting a scarf with unbelievable dexterity, looking down at her work sporadically. I looked at her and waited for her to notice. My face cried out for assistance. She could save me from grandpa, I figured. She looked back with a mischievous smile and whispered, "Your grandpa likes to talk, doesn't he, Proco?" I nodded tiredly. My grandpa kept talking, unable to hear what she'd said:

"It's not too far from here boys," el gringo said to us, "you'll be there in no time…"
Back at it somewhere in Oxnard, dusting off my overalls and climbing back onto a freight car. My

grandpa did his best to keep me interested, gathering himself, pausing between scenes to build anticipation.

"We fell asleep!" grandpa said with alarm and concern.

The year was 1993, but not to Grandpa Jose. He was back, waking up in a dark and loaded cargo. His friend was still asleep behind wooden containers. The fright grandpa must have felt unsure of his whereabouts, I thought. I was growing weary, just as those two careless riders had back then. Their field hand bodies lured to rest by the slumbering effects of a machine of locomotion.

"When we woke we started pounding the door frantically," he said, making a fist and hammering the air. "We kept yelling: Open the door!" A wetback trapped on a train in the United States is never a good position to be in, I thought.

"You know who finally opened the door for us?" he asked.

I almost blurted out the answer. The respect I learned for my elders barely bested my impulsivity. I'd traveled from California to Chihuahua, Mexico with my family. The entire point of the trip was for me to reconnect with my roots. I was a six-year-old when my family left for the U.S. Ten years had passed. As a condition of our immigration application we'd waited this long to return.

"Who opened the door, grandpa?" I asked.

"It was that same gringo! And he was laughing, ha, ha, ha!" He held his belly and used the couch springs to bounce in place, showing me how the hick had laughed at them. It didn't seem plausible to me. Trains have to keep to a schedule. And I guess it could've rode up the line, stopped in Santa Paula for some time, and then gone back down the line, stopping again in Oxnard. In all likelihood, the engine never left the station. The two men must have slept soundly for the night. Who was I to question a sixty-year-old memory?

Grandpa had come to the end of his line.

"We had returned to Oxnard," he said uttering his grand finale with poise and relief. "*Gracias a dios* we were okay."

I too was relieved. I'd heard the freight train story for the last time. We were driving home to California the following day. I looked back at my *abuelo*. He sat legs crossed and with his arms neatly folded. His head hung low. His face pensively staring. He must be contemplating his next topic, I thought. Inevitably, he shared it out-loud: "*Oye*, Luz," he said, "what ever happened to that *muchachito*, that little boy you used to call, Proco? Remember how he'd follow me around?"

I looked at my *abuela*, stunned.

"Goodness, Jose," she said apologetically. "He's sitting right next to you!"

About the Author

C. (Carlos) Osvaldo Gomez was born in Delicias, Chihuahua, Mexico in 1976. In 1983, he immigrated to the United States with his mother and older sister, residing in San Jose, CA. After gaining residency status, he attended San Jose City College and then transferred to UC Santa Barbara, majoring in Biological Sciences. He earned a teaching credential and Masters in Education also from UC Santa Barbara. He taught in San Jose CA, and returned to graduate school, earning a Masters in Administration and Leadership. He became a high school Assistant Principal at the age of 28 and worked as a school administrator for 10 years before returning back to teaching in 2015.

C. Osvaldo Gomez has been featured in the San Diego Union Tribune for his work as an Assistant Principal and helping troubled teens. He's also been featured on Money Magazine with his wife and children for having amassed over a million dollars in net worth before 40 years of age. He is a freelance blogger, writing educational articles for Lumos Learning. He's also a personal finance blogger at www.commoncoremoney.com. He considers starting a family as his greatest achievement.